Praise for David Grossman's

A HORSE WALKS INTO A BAR

"Arresting. . . . Grossman seems to be channeling Philip Roth, circa *Portnoy's Complaint,* with a colloquial voice that badgers, bullies, berates and beseeches." —*San Francisco Chronicle*

"A short, shocking masterpiece . . . in which absurdity and humour are used to probe the darkest corners of the human condition." —*The Sunday Times* (London)

"[A] pitch-black comedy. . . . It takes an author of Mr. Grossman's stature to channel not a failed stand-up but a shockingly effective one, and to give him salty, scabrous gags that—in Jessica Cohen's savoury translation—raise a guilty laugh." —*The Economist*

"Grossman has once more proved himself as one of Israel's finest literary alchemists. . . . An unsettling, cathartic, confessional stream-of-consciousness soliloquy." —*Haaretz*

David Grossman

A HORSE WALKS INTO A BAR

David Grossman was born in Jerusalem. He is the author of numerous works of fiction, nonfiction, and children's literature. His writing has appeared in *The New Yorker* and has been translated into more than forty languages. He is the recipient of many prizes, including the French Chevalier de l'Ordre des Arts et des Lettres, the Buxtehuder Bulle in Germany, Rome's Premio per la Pace e l'Azione Umanitaria, the Premio Ischia international award for journalism, Israel's Emet Prize, and the Albatross Prize given by the Günter Grass Foundation.

Jessica Cohen was born in England, raised in Israel, and now lives in the United States. She has translated contemporary Israeli fiction, nonfiction, and other creative works, including David Grossman's *To the End of the Land* and *Falling Out of Time*.

INTERNATIONAL

ALSO BY DAVID GROSSMAN

A HORSE WALKS INTO A BAR

A HORSE WALKS INTO A BAR

A NOVEL

David Grossman

Translated by Jessica Cohen

VINTAGE INTERNATIONAL
VINTAGE BOOKS
A Division of Penguin Random House LLC
New York

FIRST VINTAGE INTERNATIONAL EDITION, JANUARY 2018

English translation copyright © 2017 by Jessica Cohen

The Library of Congress has cataloged the Knopf edition as follows:
Names: Grossman, David, author. | Cohen, Jessica (Translator)
Title: A horse walks into a bar / by David Grossman ; translated by Jessica Cohen.
Other titles: Sus eḥad nikhnas le-bar. English
Description: New York : Alfred A. Knopf, [2016]
Identifiers: LCCN 2016014688 | Classification: LCC PJ5054.G728 S8813 2016 |
DDC 892.48/602—dc23
LC record available at https://lccn.loc.gov/2016014688

Vintage International Trade Paperback ISBN: 978-1-101-97349-3
eBook ISBN: 978-0-451-49398-9

Book design by Maggie Hinders

www.vintagebooks.com

Printed in the United States of America
4   5   6   7   8   9   10

A HORSE WALKS INTO A BAR

GOOD EVENING! GOOD EVENING! Good evening to the majestic city of Ceasariyaaaaaah!"

The stage is empty. The thundering shout echoes from the wings. The audience slowly quiets down and grins expectantly. A short, slight, bespectacled man lurches onto the stage from a side door as if he'd been kicked through it. He takes a few faltering steps, trips, brakes himself on the wood floor with both hands, then sharply juts his rear end straight up. Scattered laughter and applause from the audience. People are still filing into the club, chatting loudly. "Ladies and gentlemen!" announces a tight-lipped man standing at the lighting console. "Put your hands together for Dovaleh G!" The man onstage still crouches like a monkey, his big glasses askew on his nose. He slowly turns to face the room and scans it with a long, unblinking look.

"Oh, wait a minute," he grumbles, "this isn't Caesarea, is it?" Sounds of laughter. He slowly straightens up and dusts his hands off. "Looks like my agent fucked me again." A few audience members call out, and he stares at them in horror: "Say what? Come again? You, table seven, yeah, with the new lips—

they look great, by the way." The woman giggles and covers her mouth with one hand. The performer stands at the edge of the stage, swaying back and forth slightly. "Get serious now, honey, did you really say *Netanya*?" His eyes widen, almost filling the lenses of his glasses: "Let me get this straight. Are you going to sit there and declare, so help you God, that I am actually for real in Netanya at this very minute, and I'm not even wearing a flak jacket?" He crosses his hands over his crotch in terror. The crowd roars with joy. A few people whistle. Some more couples amble in, followed by a rowdy group of young men who look like soldiers on furlough. The small club fills up. Acquaintances wave to one another. Three waitresses in short shorts and neon-purple tank tops emerge from the kitchen and scatter among the tables.

"Listen, Lips"—he smiles at the woman at table seven— "we're not done yet. Let's talk about it. I mean, you look like a pretty serious young lady, I gotta say, and you certainly have an original fashion sense, if I'm correctly reading the fascinating hairdo that must have been done by—let me guess: the designer who gave us the Temple Mount mosque *and* the nuclear reactor in Dimona?" Laughter in the audience. "And if I'm not mistaken, I detect the faint whiff of a shitload of money emanating from your direction. Am I right or am I right? Heh? Eau de one percent? No? Not at all? I'm asking because I also note a magnificent dose of Botox, not to mention an out-of-control breast reduction. If you ask me, that surgeon should have his hands cut off."

The woman crosses her arms over her body, hides her face, and lets out shrieks of delight through her fingers. As he talks, the man strides quickly from one side of the stage to the other, rubbing his hands together and scanning the crowd.

He wears platform cowboy boots, and as he moves the heels make a dry tapping sound. "What I'm trying to understand, honey," he yells without looking at her, "is how an intelligent lady like yourself doesn't realize that this is the kind of thing you have to tell someone carefully, judiciously, considerately. You don't just slam someone with 'You're in Netanya.' *Bam!* What's the matter with you? You gotta give a guy some warning, especially when he's so skinny." He lifts up his faded T-shirt and a gasp passes through the room. "Ain't it so?" He turns his bare chest to the people sitting on either side of the stage and flashes a big grin. "See this? Skin and bones. Mostly cartilage. I swear to God, if I was a horse I'd be glue by now, you know what I'm saying?" Embarrassed giggles and repulsed exhalations in response. "All I'm saying, sister," he turns back to the woman, "is next time, when you give someone this kind of news, you need to do it carefully. Anesthetize him first. Numb him up, for God's sake. You gently numb his earlobe, like this: *Congratulations, Dovaleh, O handsomest of men, you've won! You've been chosen to take part in a special experiment on the coastal plain, nothing too long, ninety minutes, at most two hours, which has been determined to be the maximum permissible time for nonhazardous exposure to this location for the average person.*"

The audience laughs and the man is surprised. "Why are you dumbasses laughing? That joke was about you!" They laugh even harder. "Wait a minute, just so we're clear, did they already tell you you're just the opening audience, before we bring in the real one?" Whistles, snorts of laughter, a few boos from some parts of the room, a couple of fists thumping on tables, but most of the crowd is amused. A tall, slender couple comes in, both with soft golden locks falling over their foreheads. They're a young boy and girl, or maybe two boys, clad in shiny black, with motorcycle helmets under their arms. The man onstage glances at them and a little wrinkle arches above his eye.

He moves constantly. Every few minutes he launches a quick punch into the air, then dodges his invisible opponent, deceptive and swift like a skilled boxer. The audience loves it. He tents his hand over his eyes and scans the darkened room.

I'm the one he's looking for.

"Between you and me, pals, I should be putting my hand to my heart now and assuring you that I'm crazy—I mean *crazy!*—about Netanya, right?" "Right!" a few young audience members shout. "I should be explaining how I'm just so into being here with you on a Thursday evening in your charming industrial zone, and not just that but in a basement, practically touching the magnificent radon deposits while I pull a string of jokes out of my ass for your listening pleasure—correct?" "Correct!" the audience yells back. "Incorrect," the man asserts and rubs his hands together gleefully. "It's all a crock, except the ass bit, because I gotta be honest with you, I can't stand your city. I get creeped out by this Netanya dump. Every other person on the street looks like he's in the witness protection program, and every *other* other person has the first person rolled up in a black plastic bag inside the trunk of his car. And believe me, if I didn't have to pay alimony to three lovely women and child support for one-two-three-four-five kids—count 'em: *five*—I swear to God, standing before you tonight is the first man in history to get postpartum depression. Five times! Actually four, 'cause two of them were twins. Actually five, if you count the bout of depression after *my* birth. But that whole mess ended up being a good thing for you, my darling Netanya, because if not for my milk-teethed little vampires, there is no way—*none!*—I'd be here tonight for the measly seven hundred fifty shekels Yoav pays me with no expenses and no gratitude. So let's get going, my friends, my dearly beloveds, let's party tonight! Raise the roof! *Put your hands together for Queen Netanya!*"

The audience applauds, slightly befuddled by the reversal, but swept up nonetheless by the hearty roar and the sweet smile that lights up his face and completely transforms it. Gone is the tormented, mocking bitterness, replaced as if by a camera flash with the visage of a soft-spoken, refined intellectual, a man who couldn't possibly have anything to do with the utterances that just spewed out of his mouth.

He clearly enjoys the confusion he sows. He turns around slowly on the axis of one foot like a compass, and when he completes the rotation his face is twisted and bitter again: "I have an exciting announcement, Netanya. You won't believe your luck, but today, August twentieth, happens to be my birthday. Thank you, thank you, you're too kind." He bows modestly. "Yes, that's right, fifty-seven years ago today the world became a slightly worse place to live in. Thank you, sweethearts." He prances across the stage and cools his face with an imaginary fan. "That's nice of you, really, you shouldn't have, it's too much, drop the checks in the box on your way out, cash you can stick to my chest after the show, and if you brought sex coupons you can come up right now."

Some people raise their glasses to him. A few couples enter noisily—the men clap as they walk—and sit down at a group of tables near the bar. They wave hello at him, and the women call out his name. He squints and waves back in a vague, near-sighted way. Over and over again he turns to look at my table in the back of the room. From the minute he got onstage he's been seeking my eyes. But I can't look straight at him. I dislike the air in here. I dislike the air he breathes.

"Any of you over fifty-seven?" A few hands go up. He surveys them and nods in awe. "I'm impressed, Netanya! That's some bitchin' life span you got yourselves here! I mean, it's no easy feat to reach that age in a place like this, is it? Yoav, put the spotlight on the crowd so we can see. Lady, I said fifty-seven, not seventy-five . . . Wait up, guys, one at a time, there's enough Dovaleh to go around. Yes, table four, what did you say? You're turning fifty-seven, too? Fifty-*eight*? Amazing! Deep! Ahead of your time! And when is that happening, did you say? Tomorrow? Happy birthday! What's your name, sir? What's that? Come again? Yor—*Yorai*? Are you kidding me? Shit, man, your parents really shafted you, eh?"

The man named Yorai laughs heartily. His plump wife leans on him, caressing his bald head.

"The lady next to you, dude, the one marking her territory on you—is that Mrs. Yorai? Be strong, my brother. I mean, you were probably hoping 'Yorai' was the last blow, right? You were only three when you realized what your parents had done to you"—he walks slowly along the stage, playing an invisible violin—"sitting all alone in the corner of the nursery, munching on the raw onion Mom put in your lunch box, watching the other kids play together, and you told yourself: Buck up, Yorai, lightning doesn't strike twice. *Surprise!* It *did* strike twice! Good evening to you, Mrs. Yorai! Tell me, honey, might you be interested in letting us in, just between friends, on what mischievous surprise you're preparing for your husband's special day? I mean, I look at you and I know exactly what's going through your mind right now: 'Because it's your birthday, Yorai darling, I'll say yes tonight, but don't you dare do to me what you tried on July 10, 1986!'" The audience falls about, including the lady, who is convulsed, her face contorted with laughter. "Now tell me, Mrs. Yorai"—he lowers his voice to a whisper—"just between you and me, do you really think your necklaces and chains can hide all those chins? No, seriously, does it seem fair to you, in these days of national austerity, when plenty of young couples in Israel have to make do with one chin"—he strokes his own receding chin, which at times gives him the appearance of a frightened rodent—"and you're just coasting along happily with two—no, wait: three! Lady, the skin of that goiter alone is enough for a whole new row of tents down at Occupy Tel Aviv!"

A few scattered laughs. The lady's grin is stretched thin over her teeth.

"And by the way, Netanya, since we're on the topic of my theory of economics, I would like to note at this point and for the avoidance of doubt that I am all for a comprehensive reform of the capital market." He stops, breathless, puts his hands on his hips, and snorts. "I'm a genius, I'm telling you, words come out of my mouth that even I don't understand. Listen up, I've been convinced for at least the past ten minutes that taxation should be calculated solely according to the payer's weight— a flesh tax!" Another glance in my direction, a lingering look, almost alarmed, trying to extricate from within me the gaunt boy he remembers. "What could be more just than that, I ask you? It's the most reasonable thing in the world!" He lifts his shirt up again, this time rolling it slowly, seductively, exposing us to a sunken belly with a horizontal scar, a narrow chest, and frighteningly prominent ribs, the taut skin shriveled and dotted with ulcers. "It could go by chins, like we said, but as far as I'm concerned, we could have tax brackets." His shirt is still hiked up. Some people stare reluctantly, others turn away and let out soft whistles. He considers the responses with bare, ravenous fervor. "I demand a progressive flesh tax! Assessments shall be based on spare tires, potbellies, asses, thighs, cellulite, man boobs, and that bit that dangles up here on women's arms! The good thing about my method is there's no finagling and no misinterpreting: you gain the weight, you pay the rate!" He finally lets his shirt drop. "But seriously, for the life of me I cannot understand what's up with taking taxes from people who make money. Where's the logic in that? Listen, Netanya, and listen closely: taxes should only be levied on people who the state has reasonable cause to believe are happy. People who smile to themselves, people who are young, healthy, optimistic, who whistle in the daytime, who get laid at night. *Those* are the only shitheads who should be paying taxes, and they should be stripped of everything they own!"

Most of the audience claps supportively, but a few, mostly the younger people, round their lips and boo. He wipes the sweat off his forehead and cheeks with a huge red circus-clown handkerchief and lets the two groups bicker among themselves for a while, to everyone's delight. Meanwhile, he gets his breath back, shades his eyes, and looks for me again, insisting on my eyes. Here it is now—a shared flicker that no one but the two of us, I hope, can detect. You came, his look says. Look what time has done to us, here I am before you, show me no mercy.

He quickly turns away and puts his hand up to quiet the audience. "What? I couldn't hear you. Speak up, table nine! Yes, but first I just want you to explain how you people do that, because I've never been able to figure it out. What do you mean, do what? That thing where you join your eyebrows together! No, honestly, tell us, do you sew one to the other? Do they teach you how to do it at your ethnic boot camp?" He pauses for an instant, then barrels ahead: "Talking about browbeating, my father was a hard-line Revisionist. He idolized Jabotinsky—

respect!" A few vigorous, defiant rounds of applause come from some tables, and he waves his hand dismissively. "Okay, table nine, talk to me. Don't hold back, it's on me. What? No, I wasn't joking, Gargamel, it really is my birthday. Exactly at this minute, more or less, in the old Hadassah Hospital in Jerusalem, my mother, Sarah Greenstein, went into labor! Unbelievable, isn't it? A woman who claimed to want only the best for me, and yet she gave birth to me! I mean, think about how many trials and prisons and investigations and crime series there are because of murder, but I've yet to hear a single case involving birth! Nothing about premeditated birth, negligent birth, accidental birth, not even incitement to birth! And don't forget we're talking about a crime where the victim is a minor!" He fans air into his wide-open mouth as though he's suffocating. "Is there a judge in the house? A lawyer?"

I withdraw into my seat. Don't let his gaze take hold of me. Luckily for me, three young couples sitting nearby signal to him. Turns out they're law students from one of those new colleges. "Get out!" he screams in a terrible bellow and waves his arms and kicks his legs, and the audience showers them with whistles and boos. "The angel of death"—he laughs breathlessly—"appears before a lawyer and says his time has come. The lawyer starts crying and wailing: 'But I'm only forty!' Angel of death says, 'Not according to your billable hours!'" A quick punch, a complete spin around. The students laugh even harder than the others.

"Now about my mother." His face turns grave. "I ask for your attention, ladies and gentlemen of the jury, this is a matter of grave consequence. Rumor has it, and this is only hearsay, that when they handed me to her right after the birth, she was seen to smile, and perhaps even smile *with joy*. No waaaaay, I'm telling you! Nothing but slander!" The audience laughs. The man suddenly drops to his knees at the edge of the stage and bows his head. "Forgive me, Mom, for I have screwed up, I have betrayed, I have sold you down the river for a laugh again. I'm a whore for laughs, I can't quit it . . ." He leaps to his feet, which seems to make him dizzy because he staggers. "Now seriously, no kidding around, she was the most beautiful mother in the world, I swear to God, they don't make 'em like that anymore. Huge blue eyes"—he spreads the fingers of both hands wide and I remember the bright, piercing blue of his own eyes as a boy— "and she was the most unhinged thing in the world, and the saddest." He traces a tear under his eye and his mouth rounds into a smile. "That's how she came out, that's the straw we drew, I'm not complaining, and Dad was okay, too, really he was." He stops and scratches furiously at the tufts of hair on the sides of his head. "Um . . . Give me a sec and I'll find something for you . . . Yes! He was a fantastic barber, and when he did my hair he didn't even charge me, even though that was against his principles."

He glances at me again, to see if I'm laughing. But I don't even try to pretend. I order a beer and a vodka chaser. What was it he said? You need some numbing to get through this.

Numbing? A general anesthetic is what I need.

He resumes his frantic darting around. Like he's prodding himself onward. A single spotlight illuminates him from above, and vibrant shadows accompany his body. His motion is reflected, with a strange delay, on the curves of a large copper urn positioned by the wall behind him, perhaps a remnant from some play that was once produced here.

"Talking about my birth, Netanya, let's dedicate a moment to that cosmic event. Because me—and I'm not talking about now, when I'm at the pinnacle of the entertainment business, a wildly popular sex symbol . . ." He lingers, nodding with his mouth wide open, allowing them to finish up their laughter. "No, I mean back-in-the-day me, at the dawn of my history, when I was a kid. Back then, I was super screwed up. They put all the wires together in my head the wrong way, you cannot believe what a weirdo I was. No, really"—he smiles—"want some laughs, Netanya? Do you really want to laugh?" Then he scolds himself: "What a stupid-ass question! Helloooo! It's a stand-up show! Do you still not get that? *Putz!*" He gives his forehead a loud, unfathomably powerful smack. "That's what they're here for! They're here to laugh at you! Not so, my friends?"

It was an awful blow, that slap. An outburst of unexpected violence, a leakage of murky information that belonged somewhere completely different. The room is silent. Someone crushes a hard candy between his teeth and the sound reverberates through the club. Why did he insist that I come? What does he need a hired gun for, I wonder, when he's doing such an excellent job himself?

"I got a story for you," he calls out as if that slap never happened. As if there were no white splotch on his forehead turning red, as if his glasses were not bent. "Once, when I was maybe twelve, I decided I was going to find out what happened nine months before I was born that turned my dad on so much that he jumped my mom like that. And just so you understand, other than me there was no evidence of any volcanic activity in his pants. Not that he didn't love her. Let me tell you, all that man did in his life from the second he opened his eyes in the morning till he went to bed, all his futzing around with the warehouses and the mopeds and the spare parts and the rags and the zippers and the thingamajigs—just pretend you know what I'm talking about, okay? Nice city, Netanya, nice city—all that crap, for him, more than making a living, more than anything, was to impress her. He just wanted to make her smile at him and stroke his head: Good doggy, good doggy. Some men write poetry to their beloveds, right?" "Right," a few people answer, still startled. "And some guys serenade them, right?" "Right!" a few more feeble voices chime in. "And some guys, I don't know . . . they buy them diamonds, or a penthouse, an SUV, designer enemas, right?" "Right!" several voices shout, eager to please now. "And then there are the ones like Daddy-o, who buy two hundred pairs of fake jeans from an old Romanian woman on Allenby Street and sell them from the back room of the barbershop as original Levi's, and all for what? So he can show her in his little notebook that night how many pennies he made off—"

He stops, his eyes wander around the room, and for a moment, inexplicably, the audience holds its breath as if having seen something along with him.

"But really touch her, the way a man touches a woman, even a little pat on the ass in the hallway, just a schmeer—*that,* I never saw him do. So you tell me, my friends. After all, you're smart people, you chose to live in Netanya. Explain to me, then, why he never touched her. Hey? God only fucking knows. Wait, what—?" He perches on his tiptoes and flutters his eyelids at the audience with an emotional, grateful look. "You really want to hear about this? You're really in the mood for a bunch of shaggy-dog stories about my royal family?" Here the audience is divided: some cheer encouragingly, others yell at him to start telling jokes already. The two pale bikers in black leather drum their hands on the table and make their beer glasses jump around. It's hard to know which side they're on; perhaps they just enjoy fanning the flames. I still can't tell if they're two boys, or a boy and a girl, or two girls.

"Not true! Really? You're really and truly up for *Days of Our Lives: The Greenstein Saga*? No, no, let me get this straight, Netanya, is this some kind of attempt to crack the riddle of my magnetic personality?" He flashes me an amused, teasing look. "You really think you can succeed where every researcher and biographer has crapped out?" Virtually the whole audience applauds. "Then you really *are* my friends! We're BFFs, Netanya! Sister cities!" He melts and opens his eyes wide in a look of boundless innocence. The crowd rolls around laughing. People grin at one another. A few stray smiles even make their way to me.

He stands downstage, the sharp points of his boots protruding over the edge, and counts the hypotheses on his fingers: "Number one: Maybe he worshipped her so much, my dad, that he was afraid to touch her? Number two: Maybe she was grossed out by him walking around the house with a black hairnet on after he washed his hair? Number three: Maybe it was because of her Holocaust, and the fact that he wasn't in it, not even as an extra? I mean, the guy not only did not get murdered, he wasn't even *injured* in the Holocaust! Number four: Maybe you and I are not quite ready for our parents to meet yet?" Laughter in the audience, and he—the comic, the clown—darts around the stage again. The knees of his jeans are ripped, but he boasts a pair of red suspenders with gold clips, and his cowboy boots are adorned with silver sheriff stars. Now I notice a sparse little braid dangling on the back of his neck.

"Long story short, just to finish this up so we can get the show on the road, yours truly opened up a calendar, flipped back exactly nine months from his birth, found the date, and quickly ran off to the pile of Revisionist newsletters my dad collected—took up half a room in our house, that Revisionism; the other half was for the rags and the jeans and the Hula-Hoops and the ultraviolet cockroach killers. Just pretend—"

"—you understand," a few voices from the bar jubilantly complete his flourish.

"Nice city, Netanya." Even when he laughs, his look is calculating and joyless, seeming to monitor the conveyor belt on which the jokes emerge from his mouth. "And the three of us, I mean the biological matter of our family, we squeezed into the room and a half that was left, and by the way, he wouldn't let us throw out a single page of that party newsletter: 'Mark my words, this will become the bible of future generations!' he used to say, wagging his finger, and his little mustache would perk up like someone had electrified his balls. And there, on exactly that date, nine months before I hatched and forever upended the ecological balance, what do you think yours truly came across? The Sinai Campaign, on the nose! Do you see where I'm going with this? Isn't it some crazy shit, you guys? Abdel Nasser announces he's nationalizing the Suez, the canal is slammed shut in our face, and my dad, Hezkel Greenstein of Jerusalem, five foot two, hairy as an ape, and with lips like a girl's, doesn't even take one second to consider before he goes off to open her up! So really, if you think about it, you could say that I'm a retaliatory operation. You know what I mean? I'm payback! You dig me? We had the Sinai Campaign, the Battle of Karameh, Operation Entebbe, Operation whatever-the-fuck-else, and then we had the Greenstein Campaign, which is still partially classified, so I cannot divulge all the details, but we happen to have here tonight a rare recording from the war room, though the audio is of mediocre quality: 'Spread your legs, Mrs. Greenstein! Take *this*, Egyptian tyrant!' *Badaboom-ching!* Sorry, Mom! Sorry, Dad! My words were taken out of context! I have betrayed you yet again!"

He slaps himself in the face again, savagely, with both hands. Then once more.

I've had a metallic, rusty taste in my mouth for a few seconds. People near me pull back in their chairs, eyelids fluttering. At the table next to me a woman whispers something sharply to her husband and picks up her purse, but he puts his hand on her thigh to hold her back.

"Netanya, *mon chéri,* salt of the earth—by the way, is it true that if someone on the street around here asks you what time it is, chances are he's a narc? Just kidding! Joke!" He shrinks his whole body down, crowding his eyebrows in, and his eyes dart around. "There isn't someone from the Alperon family here by any chance, is there, so we can pay him our respects? Or the Abutbuls? Any of Dedeh's guys? Beber Amar isn't here? One of Boris Elkush's relatives? Maybe Tiran Shirazi is honoring us with his presence tonight? Ben Sutchi? Eliyahu Rustashvili . . ."

Feeble claps gradually chime in, which seem to help people break out of the paralysis that gripped them a moment earlier.

"Now don't get me wrong, Netanya, I'm just making sure, just doing reconnaissance. You see, whenever I have a gig somewhere, first thing I do is log on to Google Risk."

He suddenly tires, as if emptied out all at once. He puts his hands on his hips and breathes quickly. He stares into space, his eyes congealed in his face like an old man's.

He called me about two weeks ago. At eleven-thirty at night. I had just come back from walking the dog. He introduced himself with a certain tense and celebratory anticipation in his voice, which I did not respond to. Confused, he asked if it was me, and whether his name didn't sound familiar. I said it didn't. I waited. I loathe people who quiz me like that. The name rang a bell, but it was faint. He wasn't someone I'd met through work, of that I was certain: the aversion I felt was a different kind. This was someone from a more inner circle, I thought. With a greater potential for harm.

"Ouch," he quipped. "I was sure you'd remember . . ." He chuckled heavily, and his voice was slightly hoarse. For a moment I thought he was drunk. "Don't worry," he said, "I'll keep this short and sweet." And here he giggled: "That's me: short and sweet. Barely five-two on a good day."

"Listen, what do you want?"

There was a stunned silence, then he asked again if it was me. "I have a request for you," he said, abruptly focused and businesslike. "Hear me out and decide, and no big deal if you say no. No hard feelings. It's not something that'll take up a lot of your time, just one evening. And I'm paying, obviously, however much you say, I won't haggle with you."

I was sitting in the kitchen, still holding the dog's leash. She stood there weak and sniffling, looking up at me with her human eyes as if surprised that I was still on the phone.

I felt oddly exhausted. I had a sense that there was a second, muted conversation going on between me and this man, which I was too slow to pick up. He must have been waiting for an answer, but I didn't know what he was asking. Or maybe he'd made his request and I hadn't heard. I remember looking at my shoes. Something about them, the way they pointed at each other, brought a lump to my throat.

He slowly walks toward a worn, overstuffed red armchair on the right side of the stage. Perhaps it, too—like the big copper urn—is left over from an old play. He collapses into it with a sigh, sinks farther and farther down until it threatens to swallow him up.

People stare at their drinks, swirl their glasses of wine, and peck distractedly at their little bowls of nuts and pretzels.

Silence.

Then muffled giggles. He looks like a little boy in a giant piece of furniture. I notice that some people are trying not to laugh out loud, avoiding his eyes, as though afraid to get mixed up in some convoluted calculus he is conducting with himself. Perhaps they feel, as I do, that in some way they already are embroiled in the calculus and in the man himself more than they intended to be. He slowly lifts his feet, displaying the high, almost feminine heels of his boots. The giggles grow louder, until laughter washes over the entire club.

He kicks his feet and flutters his arms as if drowning, yells and sputters, and finally uproots himself from the depths of the armchair, leaps up, and stands a few steps away from it, panting and staring at it fearfully. The audience laughs with relief—good old slapstick—and he gives them a threatening glare, but they laugh even harder. He finally deigns to smile, soaking up the laughs. That unexpected tenderness softens his face again, and the audience responds. The comic, the entertainer, the jester, savors the reflection of his smile in his viewers' faces; for a moment one can almost imagine he believes what he sees.

But then once again, as though incapable of tolerating the affection for more than a second, he stretches his mouth into a thin, disgusted line. I've seen that grimace before: a little rodent gnawing on himself.

"I'm really sorry for bursting into your life like this," he said in that late-night phone call, "but I guess I was hoping that thanks to some, you know, devotion of youth"—he sniggers again—"after all, you could say we started out together, but you know, you went your own way, and you did a great job, big respect . . ." Here he paused, waiting for me to remember, to finally wake up. He could not have imagined how stubbornly I was holding on to my comatose state, or how violent I could be toward anyone who tried to sever me from it. "It'll take me a minute to explain, tops. So worst-case scenario, you've given me a minute of your life. Cool?"

He sounded like a man of my age, but he used a younger generation's slang. Nothing good was going to come of this. I closed my eyes and tried to remember. *Devotion of youth* . . . Which youth was he referring to? My childhood in Gedera? The years when we moved around because of my father's business, from Paris to New York to Rio de Janeiro to Mexico City? Or perhaps when we returned to Israel and I went to high school in Jerusalem? I tried to think fast, to find my escape route. His voice towed a sense of distress, shadows of the mind.

"Look," he burst out, "is this an act, or are you such a big shot that you won't even . . . How can you not remember?!"

No one had spoken to me like that for a long time. It was a breath of fresh air, purifying the disgust I felt toward the hollow deference that usually surrounded me, even three years after retiring.

"How can you not remember something like that?" he kept fuming. "We took a class together for a whole year with that Kalchinski guy in Bayit va-Gan, and then we used to walk to the bus together."

It slowly started to come back. I remembered the little apartment, dark even at midday, and then I remembered the gloomy teacher, tall and thin and hunched, who looked like he was holding up the ceiling with his back. There were five or six of us boys, all useless in math, who came from a few different schools to take private lessons with him.

He kept up a torrent of speech, reminding me of long-forgotten things. He sounded hurt. I listened and yet I didn't. I lacked the strength for these emotional upheavals. I looked around the kitchen seeing things I had to fix, or paint, or oil, or caulk. House arrest, as Tamara used to call the endless list of chores.

"You blocked me out," he finally said, incredulous.

"I'm sorry," I murmured, and only when I heard myself say it did I realize I had anything to be sorry for. The warmth of my voice was revealing, and from that warmth there emerged a fair-skinned, freckled boy with splotches on his cheeks. A short, skinny boy with glasses and prominent lips that were defiant and restless. A boy who talked quickly and was always slightly hoarse. And I remembered instantly that despite his fair skin and pale pink freckles, his thick curly hair was jet black, a contrast of colors that had made a great impression on me.

"I remember you!" I exclaimed. "Of course, we used to walk together . . . I can't believe I could have . . ."

"Thank God," he sighed, "I was starting to think I'd made you up."

.   .   .

"And gooood eeeevening to the stunning beauties of Netanya!"
he bellows as he resumes his dance across the stage, clicking
his heels. "I know you, girls! I know you all too well. I know
you from the inside . . . What was that, table thirteen? You have
some nerve, you know!" His face darkens and for a moment
he seems genuinely hurt: "Hitting a shy, introverted guy like
me with such an invasive question. Of course I've had Netanya
women!" He gives a full, round grin. "Beggars can't be choos-
ers, times were hard, we had to make do . . ." The audience, men
and women, slap their hands on the tables, booing, whistling,
laughing. He crouches on one knee opposite a table of three
bronzed, giggling old ladies with blue-tinted hairdos made up
mostly of air. "Well hello, table eight! What are you beauties
celebrating tonight? Is one of you becoming a widow at this
very second? Is there a terminal man taking his final breath in
the geriatric ward as we speak? 'Go on, buddy, keep going,'" he
cheers on the imaginary husband. "'One more push and you're
free!'" The women laugh and pat the air with affectionate scold-
ing. He dances around on the stage and almost falls off the edge,
and the audience laughs louder. "Three men!" he yells, holding
up three fingers. "An Italian, a Frenchman, and a Jew sit in a bar
talking about how they pleasure their women. The Frenchman
says: 'Me, I slather my mademoiselle from head to toe with butter from Normandy, and after she comes she screams for five
minutes.' The Italian says: 'Me, when I bang my signora, first of
all I spread her whole body from top to bottom with olive oil that
I buy in this one village in Sicily, and she keeps screaming for
ten minutes after she comes.' The Jewish guy's mute. Nothing.
The Frenchman and the Italian look at him: 'What about you?'

'Me?' says the Jew. 'I slather my Golda with *schmaltz*, and after she comes she screams for an hour.' *'An hour?'* The Frenchman and the Italian can't believe their ears: 'What exactly do you do to her?' 'Oh,' says the Jew, 'I wipe my hands on the curtains.'"

Big laughs. Men and women around me exchange lingering spousal looks. Suddenly ravenous, I order a focaccia and grilled eggplant with tahini.

"Where was I?" he says joyfully, following my exchange with the waitress out of the corner of his eye; he seems happy that I ordered. "The *schmaltz*, the Jew, the wife . . . We really are a special people, aren't we, my friends? You just can't compare any other nation to us Jews. We're the chosen people! God had other options but he picked *us*!" The crowd applauds. "Which reminds me, and this is kind of a huge thing—that's what she said—I'm really fed up with the new anti-Semitism, you know? Seriously, I was finally getting used to the old kind, you could even say I was becoming ever so slightly fond of it, you know, with those charming fairy tales about the Elders of Zion, those bearded old hook-nosed trolls sitting around together, munching on tapas of leprosy with cilantro and plague, exchanging recipes for quinoa braised in well poison, slaughtering the occasional Christian child for Passover—*Hey, guys, have you noticed the kids are tasting a little astringent this year?* Anyway, we've learned how to live with all that, we got used to it, it's like part of our heritage. But then these guys turn up with their *new* anti-Semitism and . . . I don't know . . . it doesn't sit well with me. I gotta say I even feel a little aversion toward it." He presses his fingers together and shrugs his shoulders with genuine awkwardness. "I don't know how to say this without offending the new anti-Semites, God forbid, but for fuck's sake, people, don't you think your attitude is just a little bit grating? 'Cause sometimes I get the impression that if, let's say, an Israeli scientist came up with a cure for cancer, right? A medicine that would finish off that cancer once and for all? Well, then I guarantee you the next day people all over the world would start speaking out and there'd be protests and demonstrations and UN votes and editorials in all the European papers, and they'd all be saying, 'Now wait a minute, why must we harm cancer? And if we must, do we really need to completely annihilate it right off the bat? Can't we try and reach a compromise first? Why go in with force straightaway? Why not put ourselves in its shoes and try to understand how cancer itself experiences the disease from its own perspective? And let's not forget that cancer does have some positives. Fact is, a lot of patients will tell you that coping with cancer made them better people. And you have to remember that cancer research led to the development of medications for other diseases—are we just going to put an end to all that, in such a destructive manner? Has history taught us nothing? Have we forgotten the darker eras? And besides'"—he adopts a contemplative expression—"'is there really anything about man that makes him superior to cancer and therefore entitled to destroy it?'"

The audience applauds sparsely. He charges ahead.

"And gooood eeeeevening to all the men! It's okay that you came, too. If you sit quietly we'll let you stay on as observers, but if you don't behave yourselves we'll send you next door for chemical castration—sound good? So ladies, allow me to finally introduce myself properly, enough with the wild guesses, I know you're dying to learn the identity of this mysterious man of romance. Dovaleh G is the name, it's the handle, it's the most successful brand in the entire enlightened world south of the Nile, and it's easy to remember: Dovaleh, long for 'Dov,' which is just like 'dove' except less peaceful, and G, like the spot, the apple of my dick. And, ladies, I am all yours! I am prey for your wildest fantasies from now until midnight. 'Why only midnight?' I hear you asking sadly. Because at midnight I go home and only one of you beauties will be lucky enough to accompany me and become one with my velvety body for a night of intimacy both vertical and horizontal, but mostly viral, and of course subject to whatever is made possible by the little blue pill of happiness, which gives me a few hours, or borrows back what the prostate cancer stole. Open parentheses: Such an idiot, that cancer, if you ask me. Seriously, think about it, I have such gorgeous body parts. People come all the way from Ashkelon to look at this work of art. Like my perfectly round heel, for example"—he turns his back to the audience and waves his boot charmingly— "or my sculpted thighs, or my silky chest, or my flowing hair. But that degenerate cancer would rather wallow in my prostate! Gets a kick out of playing with my pee-pee, I guess. I was really disappointed in him. Close parentheses. But until midnight, my sisters, we will raise the roof with jokes and impersonations, with a medley of my shows from the past twenty years, as unannounced in the advertisements, 'cause it's not like anyone was going to spend a shekel to promote this gig except with an ad the size of a postage stamp in the Netanya free weekly. Fuckers didn't even stick a bill on a tree trunk. Saving your pennies, eh, Yoav? God bless you, you're a good man. Picasso the lost Rottweiler got more screen time than I did on the utility poles around here. I checked, I went past every single pole in the industrial zone. Respect, Picasso, you kicked ass, and I wouldn't be in any hurry to come home if I were you. Take it from me, the best way to be appreciated somewhere is to not be there, you get me?

Wasn't that the idea behind God's whole Holocaust initiative? Isn't that really what's behind the whole concept of death?"

The audience is swept along with him.

"Really, you tell me, Netanya—don't you think it's insane what goes through people's minds when they put up notices about their lost pets? LOST: GOLDEN HAMSTER WITH A LIMP IN ONE LEG; SUFFERS FROM CATARACTS, GLUTEN SENSITIVITY, AND ALMOND-MILK ALLERGY. *Helloooo!* What is your problem? I'll tell you right now where he is without even looking: your hamster's at the nursing home!"

The crowd laughs heartily and relaxes a little, sensing that somewhere out there a dangerous wrong turn has been righted.

"I want you to come to my show," he said on the phone, after finally breaking into my stubborn memory. We dredged up a few surprisingly pleasant recollections from our twice-weekly walks from Bayit va-Gan to the bus that took me home to Talpiot. He talked about those walks with great enthusiasm: "It was a real friendship we started there," he said a couple of times and giggled with bemused happiness. "We'd walk and talk for ages. Walkie-talkie friendship," he continued, reminiscing in minute detail, as though that brief attachment were the best thing that had ever happened to him.

I listened patiently and waited to find out exactly what he wanted me to do, so that I could refuse without offending him too much and get him back out of my life.

"What kind of show is it you want me to see?" I cut in when he paused for a breath.

"Well, basically . . . ," he spluttered, "I do stand-up."

"Oh, that's not for me," I said, relieved.

"So you know stand-up?" He laughed. "I guess I didn't think you'd ever . . . Have you ever seen a show?"

"Every so often, on TV. Don't take it personally, but it's really not something I relate to." All at once I broke free of the paralysis that had beset me the moment I answered the phone. If there was any mystery in his overture, any vague promise—to renew an old friendship, for example—it now dissipated: stand-up comedy. "Listen," I said, "I'm not your demographic. All that kidding around, the jokes, the performing, it's not for me, not at my age. I'm sorry."

He spoke slowly. "Okay, you've certainly made yourself clear. No one could accuse you of being ambiguous."

"Don't get me wrong," I said, and the dog pricked up her ears and gave me a worried look. "I'm sure there are lots of people who enjoy that type of entertainment, I'm not judging anyone, to each his own . . ."

I must have said a few more things of that ilk. I don't remember it all, fortunately. I have nothing to say in my defense, except that from the very beginning I'd had the feeling—perhaps a dim memory—that this man resembled a skeleton key (that childhood phrase suddenly came back to me), and that I had to be very careful.

But of course even that could not justify my attack. Because all of a sudden, out of nowhere, I came down on him as though he represented the flippancy of the entire human race in all its guises. "And the fact that for guys like you," I seethed, "everything is just fodder for jokes, every single thing and every single person, anything goes, why not, as long as you have a modicum of improvisational talent and you're a quick thinker, then you can make a joke or a parody or a caricature out of anything— illness, death, war, it's all fair game, hey?"

There was a long silence. The blood slowly drained from my head, leaving a cold feeling in my brain. And astonishment at myself, at what I had turned into.

I heard him breathe. I felt Tamara shrinking inside me. *You're full of anger,* she said. I'm full of yearning, I thought. Can't you see? I have a toxic case of yearning.

"On the other hand," he murmured in a wizened, gloomy voice that I found crushing, "the truth is I'm not as excited about stand-up as I used to be. I was once, yes, it used to be like tightrope walking for me. At any minute you could crash and burn in front of the whole audience. You miss the point by a hairsbreadth, you put a word in at the wrong part of a line, your voice gets a little higher instead of lower—the crowd goes cold on you right then and there. But a second later you touch them the right way and they spread their legs."

The dog drank some water. Her long ears touched the floor on either side of the dish. She has big bald patches all over her body and she's almost blind. The vet wants me to put her down. He's thirty-one. I imagine that in his view I'm also a candidate for euthanasia. I put my feet up on a chair and tried to calm down. Three years ago, because of these outbursts, I lost my job. And it occurs to me: Who knows what I've lost now?

"On the *other* other hand," he went on, and only then did I realize how long the silence had lasted, each of us lost in his own thoughts, "when you do stand-up you sometimes make people laugh, and that's no small thing."

He said the last few words softly, as if to himself, and I thought: He's right, that *is* no small thing. It's a big thing. Take me, for example: I can barely remember the sound of my own laughter. I almost asked him if we could start the whole conversation over from scratch, like two human beings this time, so that I could at least explain how I was able to forget him, how an aversion to remembering one enormous painful memory can slowly dull and blot out huge parts of the past.

"What do I want from you?" He took a deep breath. "Well, to tell you the truth, I'm not even sure it's relevant anymore."

"I understand you want me to come to your show."

"Yes."

"But what for? Why do you need me there?"

"Look, that's the tricky part . . . I don't even know how to say . . . It sounds weird to ask this of someone." He chuckled. "Bottom line, I've thought about this a lot, I've been chewing it over for a long time, and I couldn't decide, I wasn't sure, but I finally realized you're the only person I can ask."

There was something new in his voice. He sounded almost pleading. The desperation of a final request. I took my feet off the chair.

"I'm listening," I said.

"I want you to look at me," he spurted. "I want you to see me, really see me, and then afterward tell me."

"Tell you what?"

"What you saw."

"Listen up, Netanya baby! We're gonna throw down the mother of all shows tonight! Yours truly facing hundreds of bra-tossing fans! Yeah, open up that hook, table ten, set 'em free . . . there you go! I think we heard a two-cannon salute there, right?!"

The crowd laughs, but it's a short, flat laugh. The young people laugh slightly longer, and the man onstage is displeased. His hand circles in front of his face as if seeking out the spot that will hurt most. People watch the hand, fascinated, as the fingers spread apart and ripple back together. This makes no sense, I think. This doesn't happen, people don't just hit themselves like that.

"*Putz*," he says hoarsely, and it seems as though the hand is the one whispering. "*Putz!* They didn't laugh properly again! How are you going to get through this night?" He flashes a frozen smile from behind the bars of his fingers. "These aren't the laughs you used to get," he says with contemplative sadness, chatting to himself as we listen in. "Maybe you're in the wrong line of work, Dovaleh, maybe it's time to step down." He drones on with a matter-of-fact calmness that is ghastly. "Yep, get out of the business, hang up your boots, and—while you're at it—yourself. But what do you say, should we try the parrot? One last chance?" He moves his hand away from his face but leaves it hovering in the air. "So this guy had a parrot that wouldn't stop cursing. From the minute he opened his eyes till he went to sleep he cursed the most vulgar, disgusting cusses you can think of. And the guy was this terribly cultured, educated, polite gentleman . . ."

The audience follows the split screen of joke and joker, drawn to them both.

"In the end he had no choice, he started threatening the parrot: 'If you don't stop, I'll lock you up in the closet!' The parrot just got even more whacked out and starting cussing in Yiddish, too—" He stops and laughs out loud, slapping his thigh softly: "Seriously, Netanya, you're gonna love this, there's no way you don't love this."

The crowd stares at him. A few pairs of eyes squint, preparing for the quick flight of hand to face.

"Anyway, the guy grabs the parrot, throws him in the closet, and locks the door. The parrot, from inside, lets out such a load of filth that the guy wants to die, he's so embarrassed. Finally he can't take it anymore, he opens the closet and grabs the parrot with both hands. The parrot screams, he curses, he bites, he slanders, he even libels, and the guy takes him to the kitchen, opens the freezer, throws him in, and slams the door."

The room is silent. A few wary smiles here and there. People seem focused on the man's hands, which circle around each other in a slow loop like a snake uncoiling.

"The guy puts his ear to the freezer and hears curses from inside, scratching, wings flapping. After a while it goes quiet. A minute, another minute, nothing. Silence. Not a peep. He starts getting worried, his conscience acts up, maybe the parrot's frozen to death in there, hypothermia or some shit. He opens the freezer door, prepared for the worst, and the parrot steps out with his feet trembling, climbs up onto the guy's shoulder, and says: 'Sir, words cannot express the depth of my apologies. From here on out my master shall not hear even one uncultured utterance depart my lips.' The guy looks at the parrot and can't believe his ears. Then the parrot says: 'By the way, sir, what exactly did the chicken do?'"

The crowd laughs. A big held-in breath that bursts out in laughter. They laugh in part, I think, to save the man onstage from his own hands. What sort of peculiar contract is emerging here, and what is my role in it? The pale young couple leans over on their table. Their lips protrude tensely, almost passionately. Perhaps they're hoping he'll hit himself again? Dovaleh listens to the laughter, head tilted and forehead wrinkled. "Oh well." He sighs, after gauging the volume and duration. "I guess that's all I'm gonna get out of them. Apparently you're dealing with a demanding, sophisticated crowd here, Dovi. Some of them might even be lefties, which requires a more opinionated attitude, with touches of self-righteousness." Then he riles himself up with a yell: *"Where were we?!* We covered birthdays, which as you know are a day of reckoning, of soul-searching, at least for those who have a soul, and I'll tell you that personally, in my state, I just don't have the resources to maintain one. Seriously, souls demand nonstop upkeep, don't they? It never ends! Every single day, all day long, you gotta haul it in for servicing. Am I right or am I right?"

Beer glasses are raised in confirmation. I seem to be the only one still under the influence of the hand that hovered over his face; I, and perhaps a very small woman sitting not far from me, who's been staring at him in wonder since the moment he walked onstage, struggling to believe that such a creature could exist in the world. "Am I right or am I right?" he yells again, and a few grunts and lows of agreement emerge. *"Am I right or am I right?"* he thunders as loud as he can, and they scream: "You're right! You're right!" It seems the louder they get, the happier he is. He enjoys fanning the flames, stimulating some kind of vulgar, corrupt gland, and I suddenly know in the clearest and simplest way that I do not want or need to be here.

"Because the fucking soul flip-flops on us the whole time, have you noticed? Have you noticed that, Netanya?" They roar back: they *have* noticed! "First it wants this, then it wants the other. One second it lights you up with euphoria and fireworks, the next it whacks you upside the head with a club. One minute it's horny, the next it's freaking out and geeking out and let me out! How can anyone live with it, I'm asking you, and who needs it anyway?" He fumes, and I look around, and again it seems that apart from me and that woman, who is exceptionally tiny, almost a midget, everyone looks perfectly satisfied. What the hell am I doing here? And what sort of obligation do I have toward someone who I went to private tutoring sessions with forty-something years ago? I'm giving him five more minutes, on the dot, and after that, if there isn't any kind of plot twist, I'm leaving.

Somehow, on the phone, there was something attractive about his offer, and I can't deny that he does have his moments onstage, too. When he hit himself, there was something there, I'm not sure what, some sort of alluring abyss that opened up. And the guy is no idiot. He never was, and I'm sure I'm missing something in him tonight, too, some signal I have trouble putting my finger on, something inside him that's calling out to me.

I start preparing for a quick departure. No, he can't complain. I made the effort, I came from Jerusalem, listened to him for almost half an hour, I found no youth and no devotion, and now it's time to cut my losses.

He delivers another enthusiastic tirade against "the messed-up idea of the immor-fucking-tality of the soul." It turns out that if he could choose, he wouldn't think twice before picking the body. "Picture a body, unencumbered!" he shouts. "No thoughts, no memories, just a dumb body prancing around in a meadow like a zombie, eating and drinking and fucking mindlessly." And here he illustrates, skipping back and forth as he merrily thrusts his hips and grins. I signal the waitress for my check. I can do without the honor of being his guest. I don't want to owe him anything. I walk around this world like a pincushion as it is. It was a big mistake to come here. He picks up my gesture to the waitress, and his face falls, really collapses.

"No, seriously!" he exclaims, and speeds up his speech. "Do you understand what it means these days to keep up a soul? It's a luxury, no shit! Do the math and you'll see it costs you more than magnesium wheels! I'm talking about a base-model soul, not some Shakespeare or Chekhov or Kafka—great stuff, by the way, so I'm told, I personally haven't read any—I'll make an emotional confession now, I am severely dyslexic, terminally, I swear, it was discovered when I was still a fetus, the doctor who diagnosed me suggested my parents consider abortion—"

The crowd laughs. I don't. I vaguely remember that he used to mention books I'd heard of and knew I'd be tested on in a couple of years when I matriculated, but he talked about them as if he'd actually read them. *Crime and Punishment* was one, and if I'm not mistaken there was also *The Trial* or *The Castle*. Now, onstage, he spews out a stream of titles and authors, assuring the audience he's never read any of them. I start to get an itch on my upper back, and I wonder if he's just ingratiating himself with the crowd, hawking some kind of down-home folksiness, or whether he's scheming something that will end up targeting me. I give the waitress an impatient look.

"Because what am I, at the end of the day?" he screams. "I'm a bottom-feeder, am I not?" And here he turns to me with his whole body and shoots me a bitter smile: "Because what is stand-up, after all? Have you ever considered that? Take it from me, Netanya, when it comes right down to it, it's a pretty pathetic form of entertainment, let's be honest. Do you know why? Because you can smell our sweat! Our effort to make you laugh! That's why!" He sniffs his armpits and grimaces, and the audience laughs a little, confused. I straighten up in my chair and cross my arms over my chest, because I believe this is a declaration of war.

"You can see the stress on our face." He raises his voice even more. "The stress of having to make people laugh at any cost, and how we basically beg you to love us." (These lines, too, I imagine, are selected pearls from our phone call.) "And that is precisely the reason, ladies and gentlemen, why I would now like to welcome, with great excitement and deference, from the country's highest seat of justice, Supreme Court justice Avishai Lazar, who came here this evening unannounced, in order to publicly support our pathetic, miserable art! Ladies and gentlemen, the *Supreeeeeme* Court!"

And the treacherous jester stands at attention and clicks his heels together, then bows deeply in my direction. More and more people turn to look at me, some applaud with mindless obedience, and I stupidly mumble: "District, not Supreme. And anyway, I'm retired." He lets out a warm, rolling laugh and forces me to pretend I'm smiling with him.

I knew all this time that he wouldn't let me get out of here easily. That the whole business, the invitation and the ridiculous request, was a trap, his private revenge, a trap I walked into like an idiot. From the minute he announced it was his birthday—a detail he did not mention at all when we spoke—I started to feel the suffocation. The waitress, a paragon of bad timing, brings me the check. The whole audience stares. I try to figure out how to respond, but it's all a little too quick for me, and in fact since the evening began I've been feeling how slow my lonely life is, how sluggish it makes me. I fold the check, slip it under the ashtray, and stare at him.

"So anyway, I'm talking about a simple soul." He swallows down a little smile and motions for the club manager to send me another beer, on him. "A rookie soul, no upgrades, no bling, your basic regular soul, just the soul of a man who wants to eat well and drink a little and get high and come once a day and fuck once a week and not have to worry about anything, but then it turns out the fucking pain-in-the-ass soul has demands up the wazoo! It's even got its own union rep!" He holds his hand up again and counts on his fingers: "Heartache—*one!* And pangs of conscience—*two!* And messengers of evil—*three!* And nightmares and tossing and turning from the fear of what's going to happen and how it'll go down—*four!*"

People nod sympathetically, and he laughs. "I swear to God, the last time in my life I didn't have any problems was when I still had a foreskin." The crowd roars with laughter. I shove handfuls of nuts in my mouth and grind them like they were his bones. He stands in the middle of the stage, directly under the spotlight, eyes closed, nodding as if he were articulating an entire philosophy of life. Here and there a few claps ring out, accompanied by sudden, crude screams of *"Wooh!"* Especially from the women. This man, I think, is not handsome or exciting or attractive, but he's figured out how to touch people in exactly the places that turn them into a rabble, into riffraff.

As if he can read my mind, he hushes the audience with his hand, his face crumples, and I see in him the absolute opposite of what I just thought: the very fact that they agree with him, that someone, whoever it is, agrees with him about something, seems to provoke in him aversion and even disgust—that grimace, those wrinkled nostrils—as if all these people sitting here are crowding in on him, trying to touch him.

"Now is the time, ladies and gentlemen, to give thanks to the one person who brought me this far, who was willing to stick by me unconditionally, even after I'd been left and dumped and abandoned by women and children and colleagues and friends"—he throws me a pinprick glance and bursts out laughing—"and even by my school principal, Mr. Pinchas Bar-Adon, let us all unite in prayer for the ascension of his soul—he's still alive, by the way—who kicked me out of school at age fifteen straight into the College of Street Sciences and went so

far as to elucidate on my report card—listen closely, Netanya—
*'An aged cynic like this boy I have never encountered during my entire
career.'* Powerful stuff, heh? Trenchant! And after all that, the
only one who never walked out on me and never abandoned me
and never left me in the field was only me myself. Yep." His hips
sway, and he runs his hands up and down his body seductively.
"Take a good look, my friends, and tell me what you see. I'm
serious, what do you see? Human dust, not so? Practically zero
matter, and with a nod and a wink to the hard sciences, I might
even say *antimatter*. You can tell this is a case of a man headed
for the scrapyard, right?" He chuckles, throws me a wink, flat-
tering me, perhaps asking that, despite my anger, I keep my
promise.

"But just look, Netanya! Look at what it means to be loyal,
devoted, for fifty-seven pretty lousy years. Look what it means
to be dedicated and diligent in pursuit of the failed project of
being Dovaleh! Or even just *being*!" He darts across the stage
like a windup toy, cackling: "Being! Being! Being!" He stops
and slowly turns to the room with the gleaming face of a crook,
a thief, a pickpocket who got away with it. "Do you even grasp
what a stunning idea it is to just *be*? How subversive it is?" He
puffs his cheeks out and makes a soft *pffff*, like a bubble bursting. "Dovaleh G, ladies and gentlemen, aka Dovchik, aka Dov
Greenstein, particularly in the files of the *State of Israel versus
Dov Greenstein* re: alimonial misdemeanors." He looks at me
with tormented innocence and wrings his hands. "Good Lord,
it's amazing how much food those kids eat, Your Honor! I
wonder how much child support a father in Darfur has to pay.
Mr. G, ladies! The one and only in the fucking universe who is
willing to spend a whole night with me for free, which to me is
the purest, most objective measure of friendship. That's how it

is, *el audienco*! That's how this life turned out. Man plans; God fucks him."

Twice a week, on Sundays and Wednesdays at three-thirty, we would finish our lesson with the tutor, a forlorn religious man who never looked us in the eye and had a nasal, barely intelligible way of speaking. Stunned from the stifling air in his house, crazed by the smells of his wife's cooking, we would walk out together and immediately break away from the other boys in the group. We'd walk down the middle of the quiet neighborhood street, where cars seldom passed, and when we got to the number 12 bus stop, next to Lerman's corner store, we'd look at each other and concur: "On to the next one?" We'd walk past five or six bus stops like that until we got to the Central Bus Station, which was near his neighborhood, Romema, and there we would wait for my bus to Talpiot. We'd sit on a crumbling stone wall overgrown with weeds and talk. Or, rather, I would sit; he was incapable of sitting or standing in one place for more than a couple of minutes.

He asked questions and I answered. That was our division of labor, which he established and I was seduced by. I was not gregarious; on the contrary, I was a taciturn, introverted boy with a slightly ridiculous—so I imagine—halo of toughness and darkness, which I didn't know how to shake off even if I'd wanted to.

Perhaps through my own fault, or perhaps because my family moved around so much for my father's business, I never had a soul mate. Here and there I had buddies, brief friendships forged in schools for kids of diplomats and expats. But since we'd come back to Israel and moved to Jerusalem, to a neighborhood and a school where I knew no one and no one made any effort to get to know me, I had become even more solitary and prickly. And then this little joker popped up, and he went to a different school and didn't know that he was supposed to be intimidated by me and my prickliness, and he was quite unimpressed by my lugubrious affectations.

"What's your mom's name?" That was the first question he asked when we walked out of the tutor's apartment. I remember letting out an astonished giggle: the impertinence of this freckled little gnome to insinuate that I even *had* a mother!

"Mine's named Sarah!" he proclaimed. He suddenly ran past me, then spun around and faced me: "What did you say your mom's name was? Was she born in Israel? Where did your parents meet? Are they also from the Holocaust?"

The buses to Talpiot would come and go as we kept talking. This is how we looked: I sit on the wall, a long thin (yes, yes) kid with a narrow, tough face and pursed lips, who avoids smiling. All around me runs a little boy, at least a year younger than me, with black hair and very fair skin, who can pull me out of my shell with cunning persistence and slowly make me want to remember, to talk, to tell him about Gedera and Paris and New York, about the Carnival in Rio, about Día de los Muertos in Mexico, and the sun celebrations in Peru, and a hot-air-balloon ride above herds of gnu on the Serengeti.

His questions led me to comprehend that I had a rare treasure: life experience. That my life, which up to then I had endured as a burdensome whirlwind of travel and frequent changes of apartments and schools and languages and faces, was actually an enormous adventure. I quickly discovered that exaggerations were warmly welcomed: no pinpricks would deflate my hot-air balloons, and it turned out that I could and should tell each story over and over again with embellishments and plot twists, some that were real and others that could have been. I did not recognize myself when I was with him. I did not recognize the enthusiastic, animated boy who emerged from me. I did not recognize the hotness in my temples, which burned with thoughts and images. And mostly I did not recognize the pleasure I took in the reward for my new talent: the eyes that grew wide with amazement and happiness and laughter. The deep-blue splendor. Those were my royalties, I suppose.

We kept this up for a whole year, twice a week. I hated math, but because of him I tried not to miss a single lesson. The buses came and went and we stayed there absorbed in our world until we really had to part. I knew he had to pick his mother up from somewhere at exactly five-thirty. He told me she was a "senior official" in a government office, and I didn't understand why he had to "pick her up." I remember he had a grown-ups' Doxa watch that covered his thin wrist, and as it got closer and closer to the time, he would glance at it with increasing agitation.

Each time we parted there were possibilities hovering in the air that neither of us dared to say out loud, as though we still did not trust reality to know how to treat this delicate, fragile story: Maybe we could just meet up sometime, not after class? Maybe go to a movie? Maybe I could come over to your place?

He waves both arms in the air: "Since we're on the topic of the Big Buggerer, allow me, ladies and gentlemen, at this early point in the evening, and for the sake of historical justice, to give a heartfelt thanks, on behalf of you all, to Woman. To all the women in the world! Why not aim big, my friends? Why not admit for once where our pink bird of happiness really lies, what represents the purpose of our existence and drives our search engine? Why not bow down for once and give proper thanks to the hot and sweet spice of life we were given in the Garden of Eden?" And then he really does bow, bobbing his head and upper body repeatedly toward a series of women in the audience, and each one of them, it seems to me, even the ones sitting with their partners, responds almost involuntarily with a quick glint in her eyes. He waves his arms to encourage the men in the crowd to follow suit. Most sneer, a few sit frozen beside their equally frozen women, but four or five get up from their seats with embarrassed giggles and bow stiffly to their partners.

This cheap sentimental gesture strikes me as silly, and yet, to my surprise, I find myself giving a brief, almost imperceptible bow to the empty chair next to me, which only serves to prove once again how tenuous and insecure I am here tonight. To be fair, it was just a slight nod of the head, and a little wink escaped, too, the wink she and I always shared, even in the middle of a fight, two sparks flying from eye to eye: the me-spark in her, the she-spark in me.

I order a shot of tequila and take my sweater off. I didn't realize how hot it would be in here. (I think the woman at the next table whispers: "Finally.") I cross my arms over my chest and watch the man onstage, and in his faded eyes I see myself and him, and I remember that feeling of *us*. I recall the blaze of excitement, and also the constant embarrassment I felt when I was with him: boys didn't talk like that back then. Not about those things and not in that language. In all my fleeting friendships with other boys there had been a sort of mutual anonymity that was comfortable and masculine, but with him . . .

I rummage through my pockets, my wallet. A few years ago I would never have left home without a notebook. Little orange notebooks slept in bed with us in case, while I was falling asleep or dreaming, I conjured up an argument I could work into a ruling, or a salient metaphor, or an idea for an eye-opening quote (I was somewhat notorious for those). I find three pens but not one scrap of paper. I motion at the waitress and she brings me a small stack of green napkins, flapping them in her hand from afar and smiling stupidly.

Actually, it was a pretty sweet smile.

"But most of all, my brothers and sisters," he roars, almost tearing up with joy at the napkins and the pens, "after giving general thanks to all the women in the world, I would like to especially thank all the precious things who privatized my own global sex initiative, all those who from age sixteen have gone down on me and up on me, who jerked me, pumped me, sucked me, rode me . . ."

Most of the audience is pleased, but a few turn up their noses. Not far from me a woman slips her foot out of a narrow shoe and rubs it against the calf of her other leg, and my gut wrenches for the third or fourth time tonight—Tamara's strong, solid legs— and I hear my own moan, the kind I'd long ago forgotten.

Onstage I see his old smile, charming and keen, and a little breathing room opens up: the distress that has weighed down the show from the start seems to dissipate a little, and I give in and smile at him. It's a good moment, a private moment between the two of us, and I remember how he used to skip around me, cheering and shouting and laughing as though the air itself were tickling him. In his eyes now there is the same luminance, a little beam of light aimed at me, believing in me, and it's like everything can still be repaired, even for us, for me and him.

But the smile vanishes in an instant, like it always does, snatched from under our feet, and from my own feet in particular. Again I sense a profound, dark deception, the kind that occurs in a place words cannot reach.

"I don't believe it!" he suddenly roars. "You, the little one with the lipstick, yes, you, the one who put her makeup on in the dark! Or does your makeup artist have Parkinson's? Tell me, dollface, do you think it's reasonable that while I'm up here busting my ass to make you laugh, you're *texting*?"

He's addressing the tiny lady sitting alone at a table not far from me. She has an odd, complicated tower of hair, a sort of braided cone with a red rose embedded in it.

"Is that any way to behave? I'm breaking a sweat over here, pouring my heart out, exposing my guts, disrobing—disrobing?! Stripping down from head to prostate! And you sit there sending text messages? Would you mind telling me what you were texting that is so, so urgent?"

She answers in an utterly serious, almost reproachful tone: "I'm not texting!"

"It's not nice to lie, sweetie, I saw you! *Click-click-click!* Quick little fingers! By the way, are you sitting or standing?"

"What?" She quickly hunches her head between her shoulders. "No . . . I was writing to myself."

"Oh, to yourself . . ." He stares wide eyed at the audience, conspiring against her with them.

"I have this app for taking notes," she murmurs.

"That really is extremely interesting to us all, sweetness. Would you like us all to leave the room for a moment so as not to disturb the delightful relationship emerging between you and yourself?"

"What?" She shakes her head in alarm. "No, no, don't leave."

She has a peculiar speech impediment. Her voice is childish and high pitched, but the words come out thickly.

"Then tell us what you were writing to yourself." Bursting with glee, he doesn't give her time to reply: *"Dear myself, I fear we shall have to bid each other farewell, for this evening, my little lamb, I have met the man of my dreams, to whom I shall bind my destiny, or at least my bed restraints for a week of extreme sex . . ."*

The woman stares at him and gapes slightly. She wears black orthopedic shoes and her feet do not touch the floor. A big red shiny handbag sits between her body and the table. I wonder if he can see all this from the stage.

"No," she says after thinking slowly, "that's all not true, I didn't write that at all."

"Then what *did* you write?" he yells, clutching his head in fake despair. The conversation, which at first he'd found promising, is becoming cumbersome, and he decides to break it off.

"It's private," she whispers.

"*Pri*-vate!" As he begins his retreat, the word captures him like a lasso and pulls him back to her by the neck. He dances backward, turning to face us with a look of horror, as though a particularly dirty word has just been launched into the air. "And what, pray tell, is the vocation of our exceedingly private and intimate madam?"

A cool breeze blows through the audience.

"I'm a manicurist."

"Well, I never!" He rolls his eyes, holds his hands out, fingers spread, and cocks his head to one side. "French manicure, please! No, wait: glitter!" He blows on his nails one by one. "Maybe a crystal pattern? How are you with minerals, sweetie? Dried flowers maybe?"

"But I'm only allowed to do it in our club at the village," she mumbles. Then she adds: "I'm also a medium." Startled by her own boldness, she holds her red handbag up higher, erecting it as a barrier between him and her.

"A me-di-um?" The fox in his eyes stops its chase, sits down, and licks its lips. "Ladies and gentlemen," he declares gravely, "I request your attention. We have here this evening an exclusive engagement by a manicurist who, although you may have thought her a small, is in fact a medium! Put your hands together! Put your nails together!"

The audience complies uncomfortably. It seems to me that most of them would rather he let her go and hunt a more appropriate victim.

He walks slowly across the stage, head bowed, hands clasped behind his back. His entire being signals contemplation and open-mindedness. "A medium. You mean, you communicate with other worlds?"

"What? No . . . For now I only do it with souls."

"Of the dead?"

She nods. Even in the dark I can detect the vein in her neck throbbing.

"Oh . . ." He nods with affected understanding. I can see him dive deep inside himself to bring up pearls of mockery and ridicule engendered by the encounter. "Then perhaps Madam Medium can tell us—wait, where are you from, Thumbelina?"

"You're not allowed to call me that."

"I'm sorry." He retreats immediately, sensing he's crossed a line. *Not a total shit,* I write on my napkin.

"Now I'm from here, near Netanya," she says. The pain of insult still strains her face. "We have a village here . . . for people like . . . like me. But when I was little I was your neighbor."

"You lived next door to Buckingham Palace?" he exclaims, drumming in the air, pulling out another faint trail of laughs. I caught him hesitating for a split second before deciding not to take a crack at "when I was little." I find it amusing to track his unexpected red lines. Tiny islets of compassion and decency.

But now I realize what she's telling him.

"No," she asserts with that same rigidity, pacing the words out. "Buckingham Palace is in England. I know because—"

"What's that? What did you say?"

"I do word searches. I know all the countr—"

"No, before that. Yoav?"

The manager turns a spot on her. In the twisted tapered mound of her graying hair there is a purple stripe. She's older than I thought, but her face is smooth, ivorylike. She has a flattened nose and swollen eyelids, but still, from a certain angle, there is a vague, veiled beauty.

She freezes at the pairs of eyes turned on her. The young bikers whisper excitedly. She arouses something in them. I know the type. Flowers of evil. Exactly the kind that used to make me lose my cool on the bench. I look at her through their eyes: her party dress, the rose in her hair, the smeared lipstick. She looks like a little girl dressed up as a lady, walking the streets, and she knows that something bad is about to happen to her.

"You were my neighbor?" he asks hesitantly.

"Yes, in Romema. Right when you came in I saw it." She lowers her head and whispers, "You haven't changed at all."

"I haven't changed at all?" He snorts. *"I haven't changed at all?"* He shades his eyes with his hand and examines her intently. The crowd follows, fascinated by the process unfolding before its eyes, the transformation of life material into a joke.

"Are you sure it's me?"

"Of course." She giggles and her face lights up. "You're the boy who walked on his hands."

The room goes silent. My mouth is dry. I only saw him walk on his hands once. On the day I saw him for the last time.

"Always on your hands." She laughs and hides her mouth with her hand.

"These days I can barely make it on my feet," he mutters.

"You used to walk behind the lady with big boots."

He gasps softly.

"One time," she continues, "at your dad's barbershop, I saw you on your feet and I didn't make out it was you."

People glance at their neighbors, unsure what they're supposed to feel. He gives me a blustery, annoyed look. This was not in the program, he says over our private frequency, and it's totally unacceptable. I wanted you to see me in my primal state, without any extras. Then he moves closer to the edge of the stage and gets down on one knee. Still with his hand at his forehead, he looks at her. "What did you say your name was?"

"It doesn't matter . . ." When she sinks her head between her shoulders, a little hump on the back of her neck sticks out.

"It does matter," he says.

"Azulai. My parents were Ezri and Esther, both rest in peace." She searches his face for a sign of recognition. "You for sure don't remember them. We only lived there for a bit. My brothers went to your dad's for their haircuts." When she forgets herself, the speech impediment is more noticeable. As though something hot is stuck in her throat. "I was little, eight and a half, and you were maybe bar mitzvah, and always on your hands, you even talked to me like that, from down—"

"That was just so I could peek under your dress." He winks at the audience.

She shakes her head vigorously and her tower of hair wobbles. "No, that's not true! There was three times you talked, and I had a long dress, the blue-checkered one, and I talked to you, too, even though it wasn't allowed—"

"It wasn't *allowed*?" He dives at the word with his claws drawn. "But why? Why wasn't it allowed?"

"It doesn't matter."

"Like hell it doesn't!" he growls. "What did they tell you?"

She shakes her head stubbornly.

"Just tell me what they said."

"That you were a crazy boy," she finally blurts. "But I did talk to you. Three times I did."

She falls silent and looks at her fingers. Her face glistens with sweat. At the table behind her, a woman leans over and whispers something in her husband's ear. The husband nods. I feel utterly confused. Dizzy. I write quickly on the napkin, trying to make order: *The boy I knew. The boy she knew. The man onstage.*

"So you're saying we talked three times?" He gulps down what appears to be some very bitter saliva. "Well, that's just peachy . . ." He forces himself to regain his composure, throws a wink at the audience. "And I bet you remember what we talked about, too?"

"The first time you told me we'd already met."

"Where?"

"You said everything in your life was happening to you for the second time."

"After all this time, you remember me saying that?"

"And you said we were children in the Holocaust together, or in the Bible, or with the cavemen, you couldn't remember exactly, and that's where we met the first time, and you were a theater actor and I was a dancer—"

"Ladies and *gen*-tlemen!" he interrupts her, leaps to his feet and quickly walks away. "We have here a rare character witness on behalf of yours truly from when he was a kiddo! Didn't I tell you? Didn't I warn you? The village idiot, the crazy boy! You heard it. Hit on little girls, too! And on top of everything else he was living in fantasyland. We were in the Holocaust together, in the Bible . . . You tell me!" Here he bares his teeth in a bountiful grin that convinces no one. Then he gives me a quick dumbfounded look, as though suddenly suspecting I have a hand in the appearance of this little woman. I shake my head apologetically. What am I apologizing for? I really don't know her. I never went to his neighborhood with him because every time I offered to walk him home he refused, made excuses, told long and complicated stories.

"And I want you to know that that's how it always was with me!" He's almost screaming now. "Even the animals around the neighborhood made fun of me! Seriously, there was this black cat who used to spit every time I passed him. You tell them, sweetie pie!"

"No, no." While he talks to the audience, her short legs kick under the table as though someone is strangling her and she's gasping for air. "You were the boy who—"

"Wait, didn't we used to play doctor and nurse, and I was the nurse?"

"That's not true at all!" she shouts, and with some effort gets off her chair and stands up. It's hard to believe how minuscule she is. "Why are you like this? You were a good boy!"

The room goes silent.

"What's that?" He snorts, and one of his cheeks suddenly burns as though it has been delivered an even-more-painful slap than the ones he gave himself before. "What did you call me?"

She climbs back onto her chair and slouches there looking sullen.

"You know, Thumbelina, I could sue you for damaging my bad reputation." He slaps both thighs and laughs. He knows how to roll his laughter out from deep in his belly, but the audience, almost universally, refuses to roll along with him.

She bows her head. Wiggles her fingers under the table in precise little movements. The fingers of one hand face the other, then cross over each other, then interlace. A secret dance with its own rules.

Deep silence. The show crumples in an instant. He removes his glasses and rubs his eyes hard. People in the audience look away. An opaque distress spreads through the club, as though the whispered rumor of a distant disruption has made its way inside.

He can see the evening dropping away from him, of course, and he immediately performs some kind of internal slalom. He opens his eyes wide and makes a happy face. "You are the most incredible, one-of-a-kind audience!" he yells, and goes back to darting around and clicking his silly cowboy boots. "My friends, you're precious darlings, the lot of you . . ." But the unpleasantness he tries to blur unfurls around the closed space like a fart. "It's not easy!" he shouts and spread-eagles his arms for a wide, empty hug. "It's not easy getting to fifty-seven, and that's after surviving, as we just heard, the Holocaust *and* the Bible!"

The woman shrinks back, her head hidden deep between her shoulders, and he turns up the volume even louder, trying to drown out her silence.

"The best thing about this age is that from here you can

clearly see the sign that reads: HERE LIVE HAPPILY DOVALEH AND THE WORMS. Hello out there, my friends!" he thunders. "I'm so glad you came! We're gonna have such a crazy night here! You've come from all over the country, I see guys from Jerusalem, from Be'er Sheva, from Rosh Ha'ayin . . ."

Voices from the back of the hall shout back: "From Ariel! From Efrat!"

He looks surprised. "Wait, you're from the settlements? But then who's left to beat up the Arabs? Just kidding! You know I'm kidding, right? Go ahead and grab your compensation right now. Take twenty million dollars so you can buy swing sets and gumballs for the cultural center in memory of Baruch Goldstein the murd—oops, I mean the saint, may God avenge his blood. Not enough? No problem! Take another acre and another goat, take a whole herd of goats, take the whole cattle industry, take the whole country, for God's sake! Oh, that's right, you already did!"

The applause dies down. A few young people at the edge of the club, apparently another group of soldiers on furlough, bang on their tables.

"It's okay, boss! Yoav, my friend. Look at the face on him! What's the panic, boss? I swear, there won't be any more of that talk, I'm done, I said so, I promised, I gave you my word, I know, but it just slipped out, that's it, no politics, no occupation, no Palestinians, no world, no reality, no two settlers walking down the Hebron Casbah. Oh, come on, Yoav, just one, just one last time . . ."

I think I know what he's doing and what he desperately needs now, but Yoav shakes his head firmly, and the audience doesn't want politics either. The space fills up again with whistles and pounding fists and demands that he go back to the stand-up. "Hang on, people," he urges, "you're going to like this one, you'll be crazy about it, guaranteed, just listen. There's an Arab walking down the street next to two settlers in Hebron. We'll call him Little Ahmed." The whistles and stomping die down. A few smiles here and there. "All of a sudden they hear an army loudspeaker announcing curfew for Arabs starting in five minutes. The settler takes his rifle off his shoulder and puts a bullet through Little Ahmed's head. The other one is a wee bit surprised: 'Holy crap, my holy brother, why'd you do that?' Holy Brother looks at him and goes, 'I know where he lives, there's no way he was gonna make it home in time.'"

The audience laughs a little awkwardly. Some express their disapproval with loud exhalations, and one woman even boos. The club manager, though, giggles with a surprisingly squeaky voice, which leads to more relaxed laughter in the crowd.

"You see, Yoavi?" he says gleefully. He can sense his ruse working. "Nothing happened! That's the great thing about humor: sometimes you can just laugh at it! And if you ask me, my friends, that's the lefties' biggest problem—they don't know how to laugh. I mean, seriously, have you ever seen a lefty laugh? I guarantee you one thousand percent you haven't. They don't even laugh when they're alone, which they usually are. Somehow they just can't see the humor in the situation." He rolls out his belly laugh and the crowd starts flowing with him. "Did you ever wonder what the world would look like without lefties?" He throws a glance at Yoav and back at the audience, senses he's been given a little more credit on his account, and charges ahead. "Just think how fun it could be, Netanya, my darling. Close your eyes for a minute and think about a world where you can do anything you feel like—anything!—and no one gives you a ticket. No tickets, no warnings, no points! No sour faces on TV, no ulcerous editorials in the paper! No fifty years, day and night, of drilling our heads with occupation schmoccupation. No self-hating Jews!" The crowd responds, they're his, and he fuels himself with their heat, carefully avoiding the diminutive woman. "You feel like putting a little Palestinian village under curfew for a week? *Bam*—curfew! Day after day after day, however long you want . . ." Another glance at the manager: "Making fun of lefties isn't politics, right, Yoavi? It's just a statement of facts, yeah? Great, so where were we? Oh yeah: You feel like seeing Arabs dance at the checkpoint? *Bam!* Just say the word and they dance, they sing, they undress. I just love the joie de vivre of that exotic nation! The special checkpoint ambience really makes them open up. They're so endearing, with their checkpoint sing-alongs: *Ko-hol od ba'leeee-vav pe-e-nii-maaaa!*" The crowd is unsure how to respond to this rendition of the national anthem. "And the way they get in touch with their feminine side! *Soldiers here, soldiers there, soldiers, fuck me everywhere!*" He swivels his body, rotating his hips and buttocks to the rhythm, clapping slowly, deliberately: *"Soldiers here, soldiers there, soldiers, fuck me everywhere!"* His body is reflected in blurred ripples in the copper urn behind him. A few men join in, and the way he sings spurs them to make their own imitation of a sharp Arab accent. The soldiers sing loudest of all. Now three or four women join in, screeching, muffing the occasional word but making up for it with enthusiastic clapping. One of them bursts out in loud whoops. But the whole sing-along is not as it seems, I think. Not at all. The performer is mocking his audience, playing with them, and yet a moment later it seems that it's the audience that is slyly pulling him into his own trap, and the interplay makes them both partners in some sort of evasive, fluid transgression, and now he divides the singers up into men and women and conducts them enthusiastically, blinking away false tears, and almost the entire room sings and cheers along with him, and then—I suspect he was aiming for exactly this murky sense of partnership that prickles deep in our guts and stirs up a sticky, messy pleasure both sickening and alluring— then the conductor gathers everyone's voices into the palm of his hand with one sweep, and there is a moment of quiet, a musical pause, and I can practically feel him counting the beats to himself, one, two, three, four, and then he storms the front again: "You want to seal off a couple of wells before breakfast, my righteous friends? Well, along comes your fairy godmother and gives you her magic wand for a week—hell, for fifty *years*! Time for some retributive justice? Administrative detention *for life*? Human shields?" The audience joins in as he makes slow, rhythmic claps over his head and stomps his feet on the wooden stage and the sound echoes heavily throughout the club. "You wanna play a round of Expropriation Monopoly? Gin-Curfew-Rummy? Roadblock-Go-Fish? Simon says power on—power off! Sterile roads? Piss-on-the-produce-Ahmed-to-keep-it-fresh?" He grows more and more eager, his features sharper and more prominent, as though someone is tracing over them with a pen. "You can do it all!" he shouts. "It's all allowed! So play, my little darlings, play out all your dreams! Just remember, my sweet ones, that the magic wand doesn't work forever—it has a tiny little system malfunction. Oh, shit!" He rolls his eyes angrily and stomps his foot like a child: "Yes, the goddamn wand has a bug! But you already knew that, didn't you, my sweet peas? Because it turns out"—he leans over from the edge of the stage and puts his hand to his mouth secretively—"that the fairy god-mother is a fickle bitch. That's how fairy godmothers are. She likes to switch things up every so often, which means that, after we've had our fun and games for a while, it'll be *us*—surprise!—singing *Biladi biladi* at *their* roadblocks! Oh yeah, the Palestinians, they'll make us sing *their* anthems, and we'll chant their slogans: *Khaibar, Khaibar ya Yahud jaish Muhammad say'ud!* So sing along with me, my righteous friends! You free spirits, you! You free-range eggs, you! *Khaibar, Khaibar, ya Yahud . . ."* The audience doesn't fall for it this time—people bang their hands on tables and whistle and boo. The audience is no sucker. A tall young man with a shaved head, perhaps a soldier on leave, whistles with such gusto that he almost falls over in his chair.

"Okay, you're right, you're right!" He holds up his hands in surrender and laughs with nothing but affection and grace. "And why think about all that stuff anyway? There's loads of time until that happens, and Yoav is absolutely right—no politics! It's not gonna happen until our kids are grown up anyway, so it's their problem. And who told them to stick around here eating up what we shit out? So why get annoyed about it now? Why all the fighting and arguing and civil warring? Why think about it? Why think at all? *Hands together for not thinking!"* Pale green tendons bulge on his neck as he cheers. "Hey, Yoavi! Why not give us some more light so we can see what's going on here? Flood it! Yeah, flood the room . . . Hey there, honeys, so nice of you to drop by! I gather Adi Ashkenazi's gig was sold out, eh? Listen, are you hot? How can you not be hot? Look at me dripping all over the place up here." He sniffs his armpit and inhales deeply. *"Ahhhh!* Where are the musk traders when you need them? Turn the AC up, dude! Waste some money on us for once! It's on me! Where were we?"

He is agitated and unfocused. The hurricane of incitement doesn't seem to have helped him overcome what that tiny little woman did to him. I can sense it. The crowd can sense it.

"We covered the bug in the wand . . . *Biladi biladi* . . . Our screwed kids . . . Would the stenographer please repeat the last few sentences . . ." He zigzags across the stage and slips a troubled look at the little woman sitting with her head down. His face stretches into a toxic jeer. I'm beginning to identify the expression. A flash of internal violence. Or perhaps outward violence deeply buried.

"A nice boy, eh? *A good boy* . . . ," he murmurs, and his face twists as if his heart were being trampled. "You're a riot, I swear! Where'd I come up with you? Is this what I get for my birthday, a soothsayer? What's up with you, Netanya? You couldn't bring a bottle of Dom Pérignon? You had to go all original on my ass? I mean, think about it, performers of my caliber around the world, they get a hot naked chick jumping out of a cake, you know? This one could maybe jump out of an Oreo! Just kidding, don't make that face, come on, dolly, it's all in good humor, don't cry, no . . . Oh, come on . . . No, sweetie . . ."

She's not crying. Her face is contorted in pain, but she doesn't cry. He stares at her, and his face unknowingly reflects hers. He goes over to the armchair and sits down. He looks exhausted, defeated. Someone carps: "Let's go, wake up!" A thin man in a blue tracksuit calls out, "Come on, let's get this show on the road! Are you gonna do group therapy with her now?" That gets a lot of laughs. People start to rouse, as if from a strange dream. A woman sitting at a table near the bar calls out: "Why don't you have a swig of milk?" Her friends clap, and from a few tables around the room come bursts of laughter and calls of encouragement. Dovaleh pricks up one finger, feels around behind the armchair, and pulls out a big red flask. Some members of the audience are already laughing delightedly, and I try to understand these people who come to his shows for the second or third time: What is he giving them?

So utterly threadbare—what is it that he has to give?

Maybe it's a good thing I stayed, I think with a strange tingle of excitement. It's a good thing I stayed to see this after all.

He waves the flask around. In big black handwritten letters, in English, it says: MILK. The audience cheers. He slowly opens the lid, takes a sip, licks his lips greedily, and grins: "Ah . . . The taste of yesteryear, as the whore said when she sucked off the old man." He drinks again, quickly, his Adam's apple bobbing. Then he puts the flask on the floor between his feet and sits on the armchair awhile longer. He gives the little lady a long look and shakes his head, looking baffled. He leans forward with his whole upper body, drops his head to his knees and his arms alongside his legs. You can hardly detect the movement of his body breathing.

The room is very quiet again; the air suddenly feels dense. The thought that he might never get up passes, I think, through everyone's mind. As though each of us feels that somewhere out there, in some distant and capricious courtroom, a coin has been flipped that could come down either way.

How did he do that? I wonder. How, in such a short time, did he manage to turn the audience, even me to some extent, into household members of his soul? And into its hostages?

He's in no hurry to get up out of this strange position. On the contrary, he sinks deeper and deeper. The sparse braid falls over his skull now, which from this angle—with his body hunched over—looks incredibly tiny and old, much older than his age, almost shriveled.

I look around carefully, so as not to break a single thread.

Most of the people are leaning forward, staring at him, transfixed. One of the young bikers slowly licks his lower lip. It's practically the only movement I detect.

When he finally pulls his body out of the depths of the armchair and gets to his feet and straightens up and faces us, there is something new in his face.

"Wait, hold up, quiet! Stop everything and start over. Start the whole evening from scratch! It was all a mistake! Delete! Backspace! It's not that you didn't get it—you guys are awesome. It's not you, it's me. I didn't get how big of a break I've been given. My God . . ." He holds his head in both hands. "You won't believe what's going to happen here tonight, Netanya! O Netanya, city of diamonds, you're a lucky-ducky audience. You are going to be given a miracle here this evening. You've hit the jackpot!" He talks to the audience, but his eyes are stabbing at mine, trying to tell me something urgent, something too complicated for a look. "Yours truly has decided, after thorough consideration and in consultation with the Gato Negro generously diluted by the manager with tap water—more power to you, Yoav, my love—anyway, I've decided . . . What have I decided . . . Let's see . . . I'm getting tongue-tied. Oh yeah: I've decided, as a personal token of my appreciation for you coming out to celebrate my birthday, even though a little bird whispered to me—the whisper, by the way, is because she lost her voice, bird flu—that you might have actually forgotten that it was my birth . . ."

He's treading water. Distracting us while he digests a complicated idea that has come to him, planning his next move.

"But you came anyway, and because of that generosity, because you came out en masse to party with me, I have spontaneously decided to give you a little souvenir tonight, something from the heart. That's the kind of guy I am. Generosity is my middle name. Dov Giving Greenstein, that's what it'll say on my tombstone. And underneath that: HERE LIES GREAT POTEN-TIAL. And a bit farther down: '98 SUBARU AVAILABLE, MINT CONDI-TION. But between you and me, my friends, what do I have to give you? Money, as we've established, I have none of. Nothing but the shirt on my back—and I barely even have a back. And I have five kids, but I don't have any of them, and my biggest achievement in life is that I produced a family that is large and united—against me. Bottom line, Netanya, you get it—I have nothing. But I'm still going to give you something that I've never given anyone else. Untarnished. A life story. Yeah, those are the best stories. I'm into this, I'm into this—what's wrong, table six? What's the panic, dude? It's just a story, you won't have to work your brain gland too hard, you won't even notice you have one. It's just words. Wind and chimes. In one ear, out the other."

He looks at me again. His eyes drill into me urgently, pleadingly.

"I want you to see me," he said on the phone that night after I'd apologized profusely for my attack. "You just have to sit there for an hour and a half, two hours tops, depends how the evening goes. We'll get you a table on the side so no one bothers you. Drinks, food, a cab if you want one, it's all on me, and I'll pay whatever you ask for the job."

"Wait, I still don't understand what this job is."

"I told you. If you want, you can record me, take pictures on your phone, I don't care. As long as you see me."

"And then what?"

"Then, if you feel like it, give me a call and tell me what you saw."

"Look, what do you need this for?"

He thought for a good thirty seconds.

"For nothing. For me. I don't know. Listen, I know this is coming out of nowhere, but I suddenly felt like, this is it. It's time."

I laughed. "Let me understand. You want me to critique your performance? Or do you just want to know how you look? Because either way, I'm not the right guy for the job."

"No, of course not . . . Why would you say . . ." He snickered. "Believe me, I'm well aware of how I look." He took a deep breath and let it out quickly, as though he'd been rehearsing this text for a long time. "I would like to hear, if you'll agree, to hear from a man like you, Avishai, from someone trained to do this, I mean, someone who's spent his whole life looking at people and reading them in an instant, down to their root—"

"Hey, hey, hey," I interrupted, "you're getting a little carried away."

"No, no, I'm just trying to . . . I know what I'm saying. I used to read about the cases you tried when they covered them in the papers. I followed the news, and they quoted your rulings, and things you said about the defendants and about the lawyers, and your words cut like a knife. I haven't heard much recently, but I remember you had some big cases where the whole country . . . And believe me, Avishai, Your Honor, not sure what to call you, I have an eye for that stuff. It was like reading a book sometimes."

His naïveté amused me. More than amused. I thought about my rulings, which I honed and polished down to every last sentence, and in which I would occasionally—with moderation, of course, unassumingly—work in a juicy metaphor or a quote from a poem by Pessoa, or Cavafy, or Nathan Zach, or even my own poetic imagery. And suddenly I was filled with pride in those forgotten gems.

A picture flickered inside me: Tamara, about five years ago, sitting in the kitchen, one leg folded under her body, a mug of hot water with fresh mint on the table, a sharpened pencil tapping her teeth with a sound that drove me crazy, going over my pages "with a fine-tooth comb for sentimental adjectives and fiery images and other excesses to which Your Honor is prone." (Me in the living room, pacing back and forth, waiting for her verdict.)

"So that's what you want from me?" I laughed. I had to take a breath suddenly. "You want a personal verdict? Privatization of the justice system? House call from a judge? Not bad . . ."

"Verdict?" He sounded astonished. "What do you mean, verdict?"

"Oh, is that not it? I thought maybe you wanted to tell me something, so that I could—"

"But why would you say 'verdict'?" A cool, cutting breeze blew through the phone. He swallowed. "Just come to my show, look at me for a while, really that's all, and then tell me—but don't take any pity on me, that's the main thing—give me two or three sentences, I know you can do that, there's a reason I chose you . . ." He snickered again, but I heard doubt in his voice now.

I knew for sure that wasn't all. There was something hiding, perhaps even from him. I asked a few more questions, tried from this angle and that, whet my blade as much as I could, but it didn't help. He was absolutely incapable of clarifying beyond the vague desire that I should "see" him. The conversation started getting circular. I could sense the gradual fading of his innocent, childish hope that even after forty-some years of separation we would still share that deep, instant understanding.

"Let's say . . . ," he murmured when I was already formulating my refusal. "Let's say you sit there and watch me for an hour, hour and a half, that's it, I told you, depends how the evening rolls, and then you pick up the phone, or you could send it by mail, I don't care, it'd be nice to get a letter from someone other than a debt collector, one page, even a few lines would be fine, maybe even one sentence. I mean, you're capable of crushing someone in one sentence—"

"But on what? About what?"

He giggled again, embarrassed. "I guess I want you to tell me what this thing I have is . . . No, never mind, forget it."

"Go on . . ."

"I mean, you know, what does someone get when they see me? What do people know when they look at me . . . at this thing that comes out of me. Are you following?"

I said I wasn't. The dog looked up, smelling the lie.

"Okay." He sighed. "I'll let you go to bed. I guess this isn't going to work."

"Wait, go on."

And it was then that something in him cracked open and started to flow: "Say I walk past someone on the street, he's never seen me, doesn't know me from Adam. First look—*bam!* What does he pick up? What gets recorded about me in his mind? I don't know if I'm explaining myself . . ."

I stood up and began to pace around the kitchen with the phone.

"But I *have* seen you before," I reminded him.

"It's been years," he said immediately. "I'm not me, you're not you."

I remembered: his blue eyes, which were too large for his face and, together with his prominent lips, gave him the appearance of a strange duckling with sharp features. A quick, pulsing particle of life.

"That thing," he said softly, "that comes out of a person without his control? That thing that maybe only this one person in the world has?"

The radiance of personality, I thought. The inner glow. Or the inner darkness. The secret, the tremble of singularity. Everything that lies beyond the words that describe a person, beyond the things that happened to him and the things that went wrong and became warped in him. That same thing that years ago, when I was just starting out as a judge, I naïvely swore to look for in every person who stood before me, whether defendant or witness. The thing I swore I would never be indifferent to, which would be the point of departure for my judgment.

"I haven't been a judge for almost three years," I was suddenly driven to say. "I've been retired, I suppose, for three years."

"Already? What happened?"

For a moment I seriously considered telling him. "I took early retirement."

"So what do you do?"

"Not much. Sit around at home. Some gardening. Reading." He said nothing. I sensed his caution, and I liked it. "What happened," I explained, to my own surprise, "was that my verdicts were becoming a little too caustic for the system."

"Oh."

"Aggressive," I scoffed. "The Supreme Court was overturning them wholesale."

I also told him that I had a few outbursts at some bald-faced lying witnesses, and at defendants who had done horrible, despicable things to their victims, and at their lawyers who kept torturing the victims with their cross-examinations. "My mistake," I went on, as though I were used to talking with him on a daily basis, "was when I told one particularly well-connected and well-promoted lawyer that I thought he was the scum of the earth. That really sealed the deal."

"I didn't know. I haven't been following the news recently."

"These kinds of things are done quietly and quickly in our system. Three or four months and the whole thing was over." I laughed. "You see, sometimes the wheels of justice do turn quickly."

He didn't respond. I was a little disappointed at my inability to make a comedian laugh.

"Every time I saw your name somewhere," he said, "I would remember how we were, and I was interested in what you were doing, where you were. I wondered if you even remembered me. I watched you climb the ladder and I really was happy for you, honestly."

The dog let out a soft, almost human sigh. I can't bring myself to have her put down. So much Tamara—smell, voice, touch, look—is still embodied in her.

There was a silence between us again, but now it was different. I thought: What do people see in *me* on first impression? Can they still see what I was until not long ago? Is there any imprint left from the love I knew? A rebirth mark? I hadn't been in these regions for a long time, and the thoughts confused me and starting tilling things over in me. I still had the feeling I was making a mistake, but perhaps, for a change, it was a mistake that was right for me. I said: "If I do this, and I'm still not sure that I will, you need to know that I won't take pity on you."

He laughed. "You forget that that was *my* condition, not yours."

I said his idea sounded a bit like someone hiring an assassin to take himself out.

He laughed again. "I knew you'd be right for this. Just remember—one shot, straight to the heart."

I laughed, too, and a faint vapor, warm and forgotten, came up from those days of ours. We said goodbye with a new sort of lightness, even an awakening of affection. And only then, perhaps because of our parting words, was I struck by an unexpected blow: I remembered what had happened to him, and to me, when we were in Be'er Ora together, at the Gadna camp. For a few seconds I simply froze in terror at my ability to forget.

And at the fact that he hadn't reminded me, not even with a single word.

"But you'll have to wait patiently, my friends, because this is a story that, honest to God, I have never told in a show. Never told it in any gig, never told it to a single person, and tonight it's going to happen . . ."

The wider his grin gets, the gloomier his face. He looks at me and shrugs helplessly. His entire being conveys the sense that he is about to take a big and disastrous leap which he has no choice but to take.

"So here you go: brand-spanking-new material, still shrink-wrapped. I'm not feeling the words yet, which means that this evening, ladies and gentlemen, you are my guinea pigs. *I'm crazy about you, Netanya!*"

Again the inevitable applause and cheers. Again he takes a

sip from the flask, and his extremely prominent Adam's apple bobs up and down, and every single person notices the desperate thirst, and he can feel them noticing it. The Adam's apple stops moving. The eyes look straight over the flask at the audience. With an embarrassment that is slightly surprising and almost touching, his voice climbs up into a screech: "Netanya, the abandoned project! Are you with me? Didn't get scared off? Awesome, good for you, I need you to be with me now, I need you to hug me like I was your long-lost brother. You, too, medium. You surprised me this evening, I'll admit it, you came at me from a place I'd already . . . A place where no white man's foot has stepped for a long time . . ." He pulls up his pant leg, exposing a skeletal, bald shin of parchment skin and bones, and looks at it. "All right, well, no yellowing man's foot. But still, I'm glad you came, medium. I don't know what made you come here tonight, but you did, and you might have a professional interest in this story, because it involves a . . . how should I put it . . . it has a kind of ghost in it. Maybe you could even communicate with it, but I'm warning you—call collect!

"Seriously now, this story is a difficult case, I'm telling you. A murder case, you might say, except it's not clear who was murdered, if it can even be called a murder, and who got murdered for life." He flashes a gaping, clownish grin. "And now, without further ado, I give you the wild and hilarious story of *my first funeral!*"

He dances around the armchair, boxing at the air, jabbing, dodging with a quick feint, and punching again. *"Float like a butterfly, sting like a bee,"* he intones with a cantorial melody. From the audience come a few giggles, throat clearings signifying relaxation in anticipation of delight. But I find myself disquieted again. Extremely disquieted. Only five steps lie between my table and the exit.

"My *fiiiiirrst funeraaaaaal!*" he proclaims again, this time with a circus ringmaster's trumpeting. A lanky woman with straw hair at the edge of the room lets out a staccato burst of laughter, and he screeches to a stop and skewers her with his look: "For fuck's sake, Netanya South! I say 'funeral' and you laugh? That's your instinct around here?" The audience responds with more laughter, but he doesn't smile. He circles the stage, talking to himself and gesticulating. "What is the matter with these people? What kind of a person laughs at something like that? But you saw it yourself. You killed! Seven point two magnitude on the Dovaleh Scale. I just don't get these people . . ."

He stops and leans on the back of the armchair. "I said '*funeral*,' sister," he drills at the lanky woman. "Is it too much to ask for some commiseration, honey? A pinch of compassion—have you ever heard that word, Lady Macbeth? *Compassion!* I mean, we're talking about death here, lady! *Put your hands together for death!*" His voice suddenly ignites in a horrible roar and he runs across the stage with airplane arms and then claps rhythmically over his head, goading the audience to join: "*Hands together for death!*" People laugh awkwardly: the slogan grates on them, he grates on them as he scurries about the stage screaming. Their eyes begin to glaze over as they watch him, and by now I recognize the apparatus: he works himself up into a frenzy, and by doing so works them up, too. He inflames himself and ignites them, too. I can't quite understand how it works, but it does. Even I can feel the vibrations in the air, in my body, and I tell myself that maybe it's just hard to remain indifferent when faced with a man so thoroughly fused with the primal element inside him. But that doesn't explain the roar trapped in my own gut, growing louder by the second. Here and there a few men join in—only men. Perhaps they're doing it to silence him, to drown out his shouts with their bellows, but soon they're yelling together with him. Something has seized them—the rhythm, the madness. *"Hands together for death!"* he screams, sweaty and breathless, his cheeks burning a sickly red. *"Raise the roof!"* he screeches, and the young people, especially the soldiers, clap their hands over their heads and roar with him, and he goads them on with mocking grins, and the two bikers screech as loud as they can, and now I can tell they're a boy and a girl, maybe twins, and with their sharp features they look like two predatory puppies watching him, swallowing up his moves with their eyes. There's a stirring among the couples sitting near the bar, too, and one guy is even dancing on his chair. A gaunt, sunken, gray-faced man waves his hands wildly, screaming, *"Hands together for death!"* The three bronzed old ladies are going wild, tossing their thin arms in the air and shouting and laughing so hard they're in tears, and Dovaleh himself is erupting, he's in a frenzy, barreling his hands and feet around, and the crowd is awash in laughter, swept up in the frantic lunacy, and there are sixty or seventy people around me, men and women, old and young, their mouths full of poisonous popping candy—it starts with an awkward hum, with sidelong glances, then something lights up in one person after the other, and the shouting makes their necks swell, and within a second they're up in the air, balloons of idiocy and liberty, released from gravity, rushing to join the one and only camp that can never be defeated: *Hands together for death!* Almost the entire audience is screaming and clapping rhythmically now, and I am, too, at least in my heart—why not more? Why can't I do more? Why not take a vacation from myself for once, from the cyanide face I've adopted these past few years, with my eyes always red from trapped tears. Why not jump up on a chair and erupt into shouts of *hands together for death*, the death that managed to snatch away from me, in six short fucking weeks, the one person I really and truly loved with a lust for life, with the joy of life, from the minute I saw your face, your round, light-filled face, with its beautiful, wise, pure forehead, with its roots of strong, dense hair, which I stupidly believed testified to your strong grip on life, and your broad, large, generous, dancing body—don't you dare erase even one of those adjectives—you were such medicine for me, such medicine for the dry bachelorhood that had closed in on me, and for the "judicial temperament" that had all but replaced my personality, and for all the antibodies to life that had built up in my blood through all the years without you, until you came, everything about you came—

You—I still have an actual physical aversion to giving the words final validity, in writing, even if it's only on a napkin—who were fifteen years younger than me, and now eighteen, and more every day.

You, who promised, when you asked for my hand, to look at me always with kind eyes. The eyes of a loving witness, you said. And no one has ever said anything lovelier to me.

"Make babies with me, death!" he screams and jumps around like a genie out of the bottle, drenched with sweat, his face on fire. The crowd echoes him with screams and laughter, and he roars: "Death, death, you win! You're the best! Take us, death, let us join the majority!" I roar with him in my bursting heart, and I swear I would get up and scream out loud with him, even though people know me here, even despite My Honor. I would get up and scream with him and howl like a jackal at the moon

and the stars and her little soaps still in the dish in the shower, and her pink slippers under the bed, and the spaghetti Bolognese we used to make together for dinner—I would do it if I just didn't have to look at that disconsolate midget plugging her ears up with two fingers like an impervious thorn in my side.

I slouch down, defeated.

Dovaleh bends over and rests his hands on his knees, his mouth open in that skeleton smile of his, sweat dripping from his face. "Stop, stop," he begs the audience, laughing breathlessly. "You're so awesome, I can't take it."

But now that he is dizzy and emitting hiccups of laughter, they sober up and quickly cool off, and they look at him with distaste. Silence spreads through the room, and in the silence it becomes clear to us all that this man is driving himself far beyond his own limits.

That for him, this is not a game.

They slump back in their chairs, breathing heavily. The waitresses start darting among the tables again. The kitchen door opens and shuts repeatedly. Everyone is suddenly thirsty, everyone is hungry.

He is sick. I am struck by the certain knowledge. He is a sick man. Very sick, maybe. How could I have missed it? How could I have not understood? He even said it explicitly: the prostate, the cancer, and there were other heavy-handed hints, but still I thought it was another bad joke, or a way to squeeze out sympathy and perhaps a little leniency in our artistic judgment, not to mention in my verdict. After all, I must have rationalized, he's capable of anything. I must have thought—if I thought at all—that even if there was a kernel of truth in his words, even if he had been sick once, his condition couldn't be serious now, because otherwise he wouldn't do the gig, he wouldn't be up to it, either physically or mentally, would he?

So how do I make sense of this? How do I explain the fact that I—with my twenty-five years of experience observing and listening, being attentive to every clue—was so blind to his condition, so self-absorbed? How did his frenetic chatter and nervous jokes affect me the way strobe lights affect an epileptic? How did I keep turning inward, to my own life?

And how could it be that he, in his state, ultimately gave me what all the books I read and the movies I watched and the consolations offered by friends and relatives these past three years did not do for me?

His illness was staring me in the face for the whole first hour of the show: the skeletal features, the horrific thinness. Yet I denied it, even though in some part of my brain I knew it was a fact. I ignored it, even when the pain grew sharper and sharper—the familiar pain of realization that soon this man who was dancing and dashing and constantly chattering would no longer be. *Being!* he shouted with a sly smile a few moments ago. *What an amazing, subversive idea.*

"So, my first funeral . . ." He laughs and stretches out his thin arms. "Have you heard the one about the guys who die and get to the induction center in the sky, and they sort them into heaven or Netan—I mean hell? No, seriously, isn't that the greatest fear—that in the end it'll turn out the rabbis were right? That hell is a for-real place?" The audience snickers halfheartedly and people lower their eyes, reluctant to look at him.

"Listen, guys, I'm talking all-inclusive hell, the whole she-bang, with fire, and devils with horns, and those little rakes, the pitchforks, and the wheel of torture and boiling tar and all those gadgets Satan gets to use . . . I haven't slept a wink just thinking about it these past few months, I swear, and at night it's the worst, the thoughts just eat me up and I totally get what you're thinking now: Son of a bitch, why did I have to go and eat those shrimp on that trip to Paris? And the pitas from Abu Gosh on Passover? And why didn't we all vote for Torah Judaism?" He lowers his voice and booms: *"Too late, scumbags—to the tar!"*

The crowd laughs.

"Okay, so I was talking about my first funeral. And then you laughed, you shits, you heartless crowd—you're as cold as an Ashkenazi in January. I'm talking to you about a kid barely fourteen years old. Dovik, Dovaleh, the apple of his mommy's eye. Look at me now—see? Just like this, but without the bald head, the stubble, and the loathing of humanity."

Almost against his will he looks at the little woman, as if seeking her approval or denial. It's hard for me to decide which of the two he would prefer, and I also note that it's the first time he doesn't look at me first.

She refuses to look at him. Keeps her eyes away. And as she does every time he bad-mouths himself, she shakes her bowed head, and her lips move silently as he speaks. From my table it looks like she's annulling everything he says with her own words. He debates whether or not to have another go at her. Something about her, I sense, makes his blood boil. His salivary glands are already releasing venom—

He lets her be.

For a split second, a fast, pale-faced, laughing boy walks on his hands down a dirt path behind an apartment block. He meets a very small girl in a checkered dress. He tries to make her laugh.

"And that Dovaleh, may I rest in peace, was peanut sized, a pip-squeak—by the way, just so you know, at fourteen I was exactly the height I am now, and that was the end of that." He gives the predictable derisive scoff. "And I'm sure you can tell, my trusted friends, that in the realm of verticality"—he slowly runs his hands down his body, from head to knees—"I somehow failed to achieve greatness, unlike in the fields of atom cracking and the discovery of the God particle, which, as is well known, I excelled at." His eyes glaze over and he strokes his private parts affectionately: "Ah, the God particle . . . But seriously, in my family, on my father's side, there's this phenomenon where the men peak at around bar-mitzvah age and that's it—freeze! That's it for life! It's well documented, and I'm pretty sure even Mengele studied us, or parts of us, especially the thigh and forearm bones. Yes, my people aroused the curiosity of that refined and introverted man. At least twenty guys from Dad's family went through his lab, and every one of them discovered, with the kind doctor's assistance, that the sky's the limit." He flashes a grin. "But only Dad, my father himself, the sly bastard, missed out big-time on the Mengele studies, because he immigrated to Israel as a pioneer thirty seconds before it all started over there. Mom ran straight into him, though, the doctor, I mean, and her whole family did, too. You could say, in fact, that in his own special way he was like our family doctor, you know? Not so?" He flutters his eyelids at the audience, which is becoming increasingly tight-lipped. "And just think about how even though the guy was so busy, with people coming to see him from all over Europe, climbing all over each other on trains to get to him, still, he found time to meet with every person individually. Although he absolutely refused to allow second opinions. You could see only him, and only for a short consultation: right, left, left, left . . ."

Perhaps fifteen times or more, his head jerks left like a stuck hand on a clock. A rustle of grumbles and protests comes from the audience. People shift in their seats and exchange looks. But there are also hesitant chuckles, especially from the younger crowd. The two bikers are the only ones who allow themselves to laugh out loud. Their nose rings and lip rings glimmer. The woman at the table next to me throws them a look and gets up and walks out with a loud sigh. People stare at her. Her helpless husband stays seated for a moment, then hurries after her.

Dovaleh walks over to a little blackboard on a wooden easel at the back of the stage, which I haven't noticed until now. He picks up a piece of red chalk and draws a straight line, and next to it another line, shorter and bent. Giggles and whispers from the audience.

"Imagine a Dovaleh that looks like this: kind of dumb, face just asking to be slapped, glasses *this* thick, shorts with a belt that comes up somewhere around the nipples—my dad used to buy them four sizes too big for me; he had high hopes. Now turn all that upside down and stand it on its hands. Yeah? Got it? See the trick?" He stops to consider for a moment, then throws himself to the ground, hands reaching out to the wooden floor. His lower body falters as he tries to hoist himself up. His legs flutter and he falls onto one side, cheek flattened against the boards.

"Everywhere I went, that's how I was. On my way to school with my backpack dangling in front, and inside the house, in the hallway, from the bedroom to the kitchen, back and forth a thousand times, until Dad got home. And in the neighborhood, through the yards, down the steps and up the steps, easy peasy, fall down, get up again, jump onto my hands again." He keeps on talking. It's disturbing to see him like that, sprawled there motionless, only the mouth alive, open, moving. "I don't know where I got it from. Actually I do know, I was putting on a play for my mother, that's where it started. I used to perform these sketches for her in the evening, before Figaro got home and we'd get all respectable. One day, I don't know, I just put my hands on the floor, threw my legs up, fell over once, fell over twice, Mom clapped her hands, thought I was doing it to make her laugh, maybe I was, I spent my whole life trying to make her laugh." He stops. Shuts his eyes. All at once he is just a body. Lifeless. I believe I hear another desperate murmur pass through the room: What is going on here?

He gets up. Quietly gathers his body parts from the floor one after the other—arm, leg, head, hand, buttocks—like someone picking up scattered articles of clothing. A quiet laugh seeps into the audience, a kind I haven't heard yet tonight. A soft laugh of wonder at his precision, his subtlety, his theatrical wisdom.

"I could tell my mom was enjoying it, so I threw my legs up again, swayed, fell down, threw them up again, and she laughed. I actually heard her laugh. So I tried again and again, until I found my spot and my head got right. And I got calm, I got happy. All I could hear was the blood in my ears, and then quiet, all the noise stopped, and I felt like I'd finally found one place in the air of the world where there was no one except me."

He snickers awkwardly, and I remember what he asked me to see in him: the thing that comes out of a person against his will. The thing that only one person in the world might have.

"More?" he asks, almost shyly.

"How 'bout a joke or two, dude?" someone calls out, and another man grunts: "We came to hear jokes!" A woman shouts back at them: "Can't you see *he's* the joke today?" She rakes in a whole avalanche of laughs.

"And I had no problem balancing," he goes on, but I can see that he's hurt, his lips turn white. "In fact, I'd always felt a little shaky when I was the regular way, on my feet, almost like I was falling, and I was scared the whole time. There was this beautiful tradition in our neighborhood: Hit the Dovaleh. Nothing serious, here a slap, there a kick, a little punch in the stomach. It wasn't malicious, just, you know, technical, the way you stamp a time card. *Have you hit your Dovaleh yet today?*"

A sharp look at the woman who made fun of him. The audience laughs. I don't. I saw it happen in Be'er Ora, at the Gadna camp, for four whole days.

"But when I was on my hands, you know, no one beats up a kid walking upside down. That's a fact. Let's say you want to slap an upside-down kid—well, how are you gonna get to his face? I mean, you're not gonna bend all the way down to the ground and slap him, right? Or say you wanna kick him. Where exactly would you do that? Where *are* his balls now anyway? Confusing, eh? Illusory! And maybe you even start to be a little afraid of him. Yeah, 'cause an upside-down kid is no joke. Sometimes"—he sneaks a look at the medium—"you even think he's a crazy kid. *Mom, Mom, look, a boy walking on his hands! Shut up and look at the man slitting his wrists!* Ouch . . ." He sighs. "I was a total nutcase. You can ask her what a joke I was around the neighborhood." He jerks his thumb in her direction without looking at her. She is listening as though weighing every word, and she keeps shaking her head firmly: no.

"Jesus, how much more . . ." He throws his hands up and looks at me, for some reason, and again I think he is holding me responsible for her presence here, as though I had intentionally summoned a hostile witness.

"She's getting under my skin," he says to himself out loud. "I can't do this, she's messing up my pacing, I'm trying to construct a story and this woman . . ." He massages his chest, hard. "You guys listen to me, not to her, okay? I really was screwed up, I didn't know how to play the game, not any game. What are you shaking your head at, little lady? Did you know me better than I knew myself?" He's getting irritated now.

This is no longer a show. There is something here, and the audience is drawn to it, although anxiously, and apparently people are willing to give up on what they came here for, at least for a few minutes. I try to overcome the paralysis that grips me again. I try to wake myself up, to prepare for what is coming. I have no doubt that it's coming.

"Here's an example. Some guy comes up to my dad one day and tells him I was doing this or doing that and I was walking on my hands. Someone saw me on the street walking upside down behind my mom. And just so you understand—parentheses— ours truly's job was to wait for her at five-thirty at the bus stop when she got back from her shift and walk her home and make sure she didn't get lost, didn't end up in places, didn't sneak into castles and dine at kings' feasts . . . just pretend you understand. Good city, Netanya." The crowd laughs, and I remember the "senior official" and the way he kept glancing nervously at the Doxa on his thin wrist.

"And there was another bonus, which was that when I walked on my hands no one noticed *her,* see? She could walk around all day long with her face on the ground and the *schmatte* on her head and the rubber boots, and now suddenly no one looks at her all crooked like she always thinks they do, and the neighbors don't say things about her, and men don't peek at her from behind shutters—they're all just looking at me all the time and she gets a free pass." He talks fast and hard, determined to thwart any attempt to stop him, and the audience rustles, responding physically to the invisible tug-of-war between them and him.

"But then Old Daddy Shatterhand gets wind of me walking around upside down and doesn't think twice before beating the crap out of me, along with all his regular talk about how I'm an embarrassment to his name, how because of me people make fun of him behind his back, how they don't respect him, and if he hears I'm doing it again he'll break my hands, and for good measure he'll hang me upside down from the chandelier. When he got angry, Daddy-o, he'd get all poetic on my ass, and the real kicker was the combination of poetic imagery with the look in his eyes. Seriously, you've never seen anything like it." He snickers; the snicker does not work out well. "Picture black marbles. Got that? Little black marbles except they're made of iron. Something was wrong with those eyes, they were too close together, too round. I'm telling you, you look into those eyes for two seconds and you feel like a little animal is flipping the whole evolution thing over on you."

Since the snicker failed, he dispatches his infectious belly laugh to the front lines and resumes scurrying across the stage, trying to reelectrify his movements. "So what did you do, Dovaleh? That's what you're probably asking yourself now, I know you're worried: What did little Dovaleh do? I went back to walking on my feet, that's what I did. Like I had a choice? You don't mess with my dad, and in our house, if you haven't yet figured this out, there was monotheism: no God but *him*. Only his will held, and if you dared make a peep, out came the belt— *whack!*" He whips the air and the tendons on his neck protrude and his face twists in a flash of terror and hatred, but his lips form a smile, or a glower, and for a moment I see a little boy, the little boy I knew, who apparently I didn't know—increasingly I realize how little I knew; what an actor he was, good Lord, what an actor, even then, and what an enormous effort of play-acting our friendship was for him—a little boy trapped between the table and the wall as his father lashes him with a belt.

He never told me, never even hinted, that his father beat him. Or that he got beat up at school. Or that anyone was capable of hurting him at all. On the contrary: he looked like a happy, well-liked boy, and his light, optimistic warmth was what drew me to him, with magical threads, out of my own childhood and my own home, where there was always something cold and murky and somewhat secretive.

He keeps stretching out his stage smile, but the little woman flinches at the whipping hand, as though she were the one hit with the belt. When she lets out a barely audible sigh, he quickly spins around at her with furious dark eyes like a snake about to bite. And suddenly she looks larger, this stubborn, odd little woman, a self-appointed warrior battling for the soul of a boy she knew decades ago and of whom almost no trace remains.

"Okay, Dad says no walking on hands, so I don't. But then I start thinking, What now? How do I save myself? You know what I mean? How do I not die from all this uprightness? How do I *be*? That's how my mind worked back then; I always had this restlessness. Okay, so he wants to see me walk like everyone does? Fantastic, I'll walk like he wants me to, I'll stay on my feet, I'll be a good little boy, but I'm going to follow the rules of chess when I walk, okay?"

The audience stares at him, trying to figure out where he's going.

"For example"—he giggles, employing a complex mimicry of his own face to cajole us to laugh with him—"one day I'd walk only diagonally, like the bishop. The next day only straight, like the rook. Then like the knight, one-step-two-step. And I saw people like they were playing chess with me. Not that they knew it, of course, how would they? But they each had their role, the whole street was my board, the whole school yard at recess . . ."

Again I see the two of us walking and talking. He circles around me, making me dizzy, popping out here, emerging from there. Who knows what game of his I was taking part in?

"I'd come up to my dad like a knight, say, while he was sawing the rags in the jeans room—never mind, trust me, there's a universe somewhere where that sentence makes sense—and I'd position myself right on the floor tile where I could defend my mother, the queen, and I'd stand there between him and Mom, and I'd say to him silently: Check. And I'd wait a few seconds, give him time to make his move, and if he didn't step onto another tile in time, it was checkmate. Isn't that loopy? Wouldn't you laugh at that kid if you knew what was going on in his head? Wouldn't you wonder what this fuckup wasted his childhood on?"

He slams these last words at the little woman. He doesn't even look at her, but it's the voice meant for her, and she straightens up and shouts out in a desperate, horrible voice: "Stop it! You were the best one! You didn't say 'midget' and you didn't take me to the warehouse, and you called me 'Pitz,' and 'Pitz' was good, don't you remember?"

"No." He stands before her, arms hanging limply at his sides.

"And the second time we talked you brought me in your mouth a picture of Isadora Duncan from the paper, and I still have it in my room. How can you not remember?"

"I don't remember, lady," he murmurs, embarrassed.

"Why do you call me lady?" she whispers.

He sighs. Scrubs the sparse islands of hair on his temples. He senses, of course, that the whole show is starting to tilt again. He is out on a limb that is getting heavier than the whole tree. The crowd can feel it, too. People look at one another and shift restlessly. They understand less and less what it is that they have unwillingly become partners to. I have no doubt they would have gotten up and left long ago, or even booed him off the stage, if not for the temptation that is so hard to resist—the temptation to look into another man's hell.

"I'm all good! Dovaleh rides again!" he booms, and widens his mouth into that false, seductive smile. "Just picture our little Dovi, with his rainbow of zits, a fireworks show, his voice still hasn't changed, he still hasn't touched the tip of a nipple, but his left hand is suspiciously muscular 'cause what he lacks in size he makes up for with horniness . . ."

He prattles on, juggling words. For a few minutes now I've felt a hole in my stomach. A pit. A sudden gnawing hunger that I have to cork immediately. I order some tapas and ask the waitress to bring them out as soon as possible.

"Remember that age when you're an adolescent and everything in the world makes you wicked horny? Like you're sitting in geometry class and the teacher says, *Look at the two legs of this isosceles triangle* . . . And all the guys in class start breathing heavily and drooling . . . Ahhh . . . Or she goes, *Now put a vertical line into the center of the circle* . . ." He shuts his eyes and makes sucking, licking moves with his lips and tongue. The audience titters, but the tiny woman glares at him, and her look is so pained that I can't decide whether the sight is heart-wrenching or ridiculous.

"Long story short, my class goes down south to this place

called Be'er Ora, near Eilat, for Gadna camp—remember those? Where they prepared the future soldiers of Israel?"

Here it comes. Almost parenthetically. For two weeks, since our phone conversation, I've been waiting for him to get here. To drag me with him into that abyss.

"Remember the Gadna days, my good friends? Anyone know if they still make high schoolers do those camps? Yes? No? Yes?"

The emptiness of a long fall.

Five steps between me and the door.

The sweetness of the revenge I am about to be subjected to.

Just deserts.

"I'll bet you a million dollars those lefties did away with Gadna, right? I don't know, I'm just guessing, I know they can't stand it when anyone has any fun, especially when it's like military education for kids—yuck! Are we in Sparta or are we in Israel?!"

He keeps turning up the flames beneath himself. I know it already, I recognize it. I straighten up in my chair. He won't catch me unprepared.

He continues in an excited whisper: "We set off on the road! Five a.m., still dark, our parents drop us off half asleep at the Umschlagplatz—just kiddiiiiing!" He slaps his wrist. "I don't know how that slipped out, it must be the Tourette's. Each kid is allowed one backpack. They call our names out, load us on the trucks, we say goodbye to our parents, then we sit there for ten hours on backbreaking wooden benches. We sit facing each other so no one misses when they puke, each kid's knees touching someone else's—I got Shimshon Katzover's, which were nothing special. We sing our imbecilic hymns and youth movement anthems. You know, all the good ones, like *She screws her leg out every night, she drops her teeth into a glass . . .*" A few women start singing along enthusiastically, and he gives them a chilling look. "Hey, medium," he inquires without looking at her, "could you maybe put me in touch with myself at that age?"

"No, I'm only allowed to do it in the club at our village, and only with people who died."

"That should work out perfectly, then. And by the way, I didn't want to go to that camp at all, just so you know. I'd never left home for a week, never been apart from them for that long. There'd never been any reason to. Going abroad wasn't done back then, definitely not by our sort. Overseas, for us, was strictly for extermination purposes. And we didn't travel around Israel either—where would we go? Who was expecting us? It was just the three of us, mom-dad-kid, and when we stood there by the trucks that morning, honestly, I got a little spooked. I don't know, something about the whole thing just didn't sit well, like I had some kind of sixth sense, or maybe I was afraid, I don't know, to leave them alone with each other—"

He went to Be'er Ora with his school, and I went with mine. We weren't supposed to be in the same camp. His school was signed up for a different base (Sde Boker, I think), but the organizers had other ideas, and we found ourselves not just at the same camp but in the same platoon and the same tent.

"So I tell my dad I don't feel well, he has to take me home, and he says, 'Over my dead body.' I swear that's what he said, and I got even more stressed out and then the tears started, and I wanted the ground to open up . . .

"I mean, when I think about it now, it's so weird that I cried in front of everyone. Picture it: I was almost fourteen, a pretty major nerd, but my dad was the red-faced one. *He* got annoyed at *us*, because when my mom saw me cry she started, too; she always did that, whenever there was any crying she would join right in. He hated to see her cry, he always teared up when it happened, he was emotional, especially with her, there's no question about it, he really did love her, Daddy-o, in his own way, as they say, but he loved her, I admit it, he did, maybe like a squirrel or a mouse who finds a pretty piece of glass or a colorful marble and can't stop looking at it . . ." He smiles. "Remember those awesome marbles they used to have? Remember that one with the butterfly inside? That's the kind of marble she was, my mother."

A few men in the audience remember, as do I, and one tall woman with cropped silver hair. We're all the same age, more or less. People throw out names of other marbles: cat's-eyes, aggies, oilies. I contribute—meaning, I draw on the green napkin—the Dutch variety with the flower inside. The younger audience members titter at our enthusiasm. Dovaleh stands there grinning, soaking up the heartfelt moment. Then he flicks an imaginary marble straight at me. The tenderness and warmth on his face confuse me.

"It was something unreal, I'm telling you. Because for him, or at least this is how it seemed, my mother was a gift from heaven. She was something really precious he'd been given to protect, but like at the same moment they also said: Watch it, mister— you're just the caretaker, got it? You're not going to really be with her, so keep your distance. You know what the Bible says—oh, by the way, Netanya, the Bible is awesome! Such a page-turner! I give it a big thumbs-up. If I wasn't such a restrained individual I might even call it the book of books. And it's full of dirty bits!

So anyway, right off the bat the Bible says, 'And the man knew Eve his wife,' right?" A few voices answer: "Right." "Okay. Great job, Mr. Adam, you're a real stud. Except pay attention to how it says you *knew* her. It doesn't say anything about *understanding* her, eh, girls? Am I right?" The women cheer, and a band of warmth rises up from them and floats over to surround him like an aura. He grins and somehow manages to encompass them all in a single wink, and yet I sense that each of them was winked at in a slightly different way.

"He just didn't understand. My dad did not understand this beautiful woman who didn't say a word all day, just sat there with her books and the door shut, didn't ask him for anything and didn't want anything and all his finagling and hustling didn't even make a dent in her. Somehow, he managed to rent out the storehouse behind the barbershop to a family of four for two-fifty bucks a month—*ta-daa!* Then he buys a crate of velveteen pants that came in on a fishing boat from Marseille, with slightly defective zippers, and those things stank up our apartment for two years. Hallelujah! And she'd sit next to him at the kitchen table every evening, for years this went on, and she was a whole head taller than him, sitting there like a statue"— he reaches both arms out like an obedient pupil or a prisoner holding out his hands for the cuffs—"and he'd open up the ledger where he wrote down numbers like fly droppings with all kinds of code names he made up for his clients and his suppliers, the ones who were honest with him and the ones who screwed him. There was Pharaoh, and the Sweetheart of Sosnowiec, and Sarah Bernhardt, Zishe Breitbart, Goebbels, Rumkowski, Meir Vilner, Ben-Gurion . . . And he'd get all excited, you should have seen him, and sweaty, and beet red, and his finger would shake on the numbers, and this whole thing was just to prove to her, as if she was even arguing, as if she even heard anything he said, that in such-and-such years and so-and-so months he'd have enough money so we could move into a two-bedroom apartment with a balcony in Kiryat Moshe."

Looking up at the crowd, he seems to have forgotten where he is for a moment, but he quickly recovers and apologizes with a smile and a shrug.

"After ten hours on the bus we get to some place in the boonies, out in the Negev, or maybe it was the Aravah. Somewhere near Eilat. Let's see . . . I'll try and communicate with my late self . . ." He rolls his eyes, tilts his head back, and mumbles: "I see . . . brown and red mountains, a desert, and tents, and officers' barracks, and a mess hall, and a ripped Israeli flag on a mast, and a puddle of diesel, and a degenerate generator on its last legs, and mess tins we used to get for bar-mitzvah gifts and we'd rinse them at the spigot with a filthy sponge and cold water so all the grease stayed on—"

The audience is his now, dipping its feet in familiar waters. We were there for four days, Dovaleh and I, in the same platoon, and most of the time we slept in the same tent and ate at the same table. And we did not exchange a single word.

"The counselors at this base, or commanders, I guess they were called, they each had their own particular strand of fucked-up-ness. Every one of them was like a rough draft of an actual human being. The real army wouldn't take them, so they made them babysit a bunch of kids at Gadna camp. One guy was so cross-eyed he couldn't see an inch ahead, the other was flat-footed, one dude was from Holon. Believe me, out of ten of them you could put together maybe one normal person.

"Honey," he turns to the medium with a sigh, "you're turning my milk sour. Look at everyone else laughing! Don't you think my jokes are funny?"

"No."

"What?! None of them?"

"Your jokes are bad." Her eyes are on the table, and her fingers grip her purse straps.

"Bad, as in not funny?" he asks tenderly. "Or as in, like, they're mean?"

She doesn't respond immediately. "Both," she says finally.

"So my jokes are not funny, and they're also mean."

She thinks for another moment. "Yes."

"But that's what stand-up comedy is."

"Then it's not right."

He gives her a long, bemused look. "Then why did you come?"

"Because at the club they said stand-up, but I thought they meant karaoke."

They're conversing as though no one else is in the room.

"Well, now you know what it is and you can leave."

"I want to stay."

"But why? You're not having fun. You're miserable here."

"That's true." Her face turns gloomy. Every emotion that passes through her is immediately visible on her face. In fact, I think I'm spending as much time looking at her this evening as at him. I've only just realized it: I constantly look back and forth between them, gauging him by her responses.

"Please leave, it's going to get harder for you now."

"I want to stay." When she purses her lips, the exaggerated circle of red lipstick makes her look like a tiny clown with hurt feelings.

Dovaleh sucks in his sunken cheeks, and his eyes seem to get closer together. "Okay," he murmurs, "but I warned you, honey. Don't come crying to me later."

She stares at him, uncomprehending, then shrinks back.

"*Give it up, Netanya!*" he howls in her direction. "So we get there after ten hours, they put us in tents, big tents, ten, twenty guys per tent, or maybe less? I don't remember, I can't remember, I can't remember anything anymore, don't trust a word I say, seriously, my head is a sieve, I swear, back when my kids still knew they had a dad and they used to come visit, I'd say, 'Whoa! Before you go any further, put your name tags on!'"

Feeble laughter.

"And down there, in Be'er Ora, they teach us all the things a proud young Hebrew boy needs to know: how to climb up walls in case we have to escape the ghetto again; how to slink, for the sewage pipes; how to drop, crawl, and fire, a procedure we called *patzatzta*, so the Nazis won't understand and they'll get bummed out. And they make us jump off a tower onto a canvas—remember that? And walk on a rope like a lizard, and day treks and night treks, and sweating and running around the base in horrendous heat, and shooting five bullets with a Czech Mauser and feeling like James Bond, and me"—he flutters his eyelids coquettishly—"the shooting makes me feel close to Mommy, it gives me a little taste of home, because my mom— did I tell you this? I didn't? My mom worked for Taas. Yep, for the Israel Military Industries in Jerusalem. She was a bullet sorter, my sweet little mommy, six shifts a week. Dad set it up for her, someone probably owed him something and they gave her a job even with all her baggage. For the life of me I don't know what was going through my dad's head. What was he thinking? Nine hours a day, her, with bullets: *ta-ta-ta-ta-ta!*" He holds an imaginary submachine gun and fires in all directions, shouting hoarsely: "Be'er Ora, here I come! Think kitchen duty! Think giant cauldrons! And scabies! Scratching and itching like little Jobs! And diarrhea flowing freely because the chef, bless him, earned three stars in the Michelin guide to dysentery—"

It's been a few minutes since he's looked me in the eye.

"And in the evening there were parties and bonfires and sing-alongs and putting out fires the old-fashioned way—all they let me do with my dick was put out a firefly—and good times, and boys and girls, and yin and yang dancing the krakowiak, and I partied like you wouldn't believe. I was the platoon's funny guy, they laughed with me, they paid attention, they tossed me gaily around in a circle, 'cause I was little, I weighed nothing, and I was the youngest one there, I skipped a grade one time, never mind, not that I was the smartest, they just got sick of me and kicked me up. So at Gadna camp they made me their mascot, their good-luck Dovaleh. Before every exercise or firing range, each kid came over and gave me a little smack upside the head, but it was all in good spirits, it was all good. Bambino, that's what they called me. It was the first time I had a decent nick-name. Better than Boots or Rag-and-Bone."

That was how I ran into him. I got to the base and went into my tent to unpack, and I saw three oversize kids throwing a big army duffel back and forth, with a boy inside screaming like an animal. I didn't know the boys. I was the only one from my school who got assigned to that tent. I assume my Gadna teacher, who divvied us up, thought I'd feel equally out of place anywhere I went. I remember standing at the tent flaps without moving. I couldn't stop watching. The three kids were in their undershirts, and their biceps glistened with sweat. The kid in the duffel bag had stopped shouting and was crying now, and they snickered without saying a word and kept tossing him back and forth.

I put my backpack down on a bed that looked available near the entrance, and sat down with my back to the events. I didn't dare interfere, but I also couldn't leave the tent. At some point I heard a loud thump and I jumped. One of them must have dropped the duffel bag on the cement floor. It quickly opened up and a head of curly black hair emerged. I recognized him immediately. The kids probably saw something on my face, because they sniggered. Dovaleh followed their gazes and stared at me. His face was wet with tears. The encounter was beyond our comprehension, and in some ways beyond our means. We made no sign of mutual recognition. Even as photo negatives of ourselves, we were completely in sync. His scream had frozen in my throat, or so I felt. I held my head up high, looked away, and walked out, still hearing their cackles.

"And there was girls-and-boys stuff going on there, and fresh new hormones, still unwrapped, and the merry crackle of zits popping. I was still pretty green in that area, you know, I'd only just started my first experiments with myself, magazines and pictures and all that, and when it came to the main event I was really only on observer status, but man did I enjoy observing! That's where I started building the observation tower that would last a lifetime."

He smiles. People smile at him. What is he selling them? What is he selling himself?

Shortly after our encounter, I met him in the mess hall. Since we were in the same tent, we were also at the same table, although, fortunately for me, on opposite ends. I loaded up my plate and looked at nothing else, but I couldn't avoid seeing his classmates dump a whole saltshaker into his soup. He slurped it up cheerfully and made loud sucking noises, which had them all falling about laughing. Someone grabbed the baseball cap off his head and it flew back and forth across the table, got dipped into the occasional bowl of something, and finally landed back on his head and drizzled liquid down his face. He reached his tongue out and licked the drippings. Once in a while, through the jabs and the silly faces, his eyes met mine, indifferent and vacant.

At the end of the meal they stuffed half a banana in his mouth and he scratched at his ribs and made monkey howls, until the platoon commander ordered him to shut up and sit down.

At night, when we all lay in bed after lights-out, the boys in the tent made him tell them the dreams he had about a girl in their class, who was particularly well endowed. He did. He used words I couldn't believe he knew. But it was his voice, his flow of speech, his rich imagination. I lay motionless, almost without breathing, and knew for sure that if he hadn't been in the tent it would have been me they'd be picking on.

One boy from his class suddenly ran down the two rows of beds mimicking Dovaleh's father, and another got up and started impersonating his mother. I pulled the army blanket up over my head. The boys laughed and Dovaleh laughed with them. His voice hadn't changed yet, and it rang out with a strange freshness among their deeper tones. Someone said, "If I walked down Dizengoff with Greenstein, people would think I was with a girl!" A big wave of laughter flowed down the tent.

After the second night, I begged my teacher to let me switch. On the third night I lay in a different bed, in a different tent, far from his, but I still felt the aftershocks. On the fourth night they assigned me to guard duty with a girl in my class, and I stopped thinking about Dovaleh.

He was right: I blocked him out.

"At night everyone runs in the dark between the tents, and from every direction you hear *aahh* and *oooh* and *Get your hand out, you idiot,* and *C'mon, let me.* And *Gross, what's with the tongue? And Put your hand there, just feel it,* and *I really really can't today,* and *My mom will kill me,* and *How the hell do you open all these hooks,* and *What is that, yuck, what did you squirt on me,* and *You bitch, you shut my zipper on it . . ."*

His audience surges and ebbs on waves of laughter. He still avoids my look. I wait. I'm ready. In a minute or two he'll turn to me with a big grin: *What a coincidence! Such a small world! The Honorable Avishai Lazar was there, too!*

On the second morning I was sent from the firing range to bring the water canteen I'd left in my tent. I remember how nice it was to be alone suddenly, away from the noise and the yelling and the commands that filled up every inch of space, and what a relief it was to finally be without him, without the torture of his presence. The air was clear and there was a soothing freshness everywhere. (Now, as I write, the smell of the water and soap from the morning wash comes back to me, pooled in the little cement dimples of the tent floor.)

I sat on my bed. The tent flaps were open and I could quietly look out at the desert, whose beauty stunned me and was something of a comfort to me. I tried to empty my mind. And it was then, perhaps because I let down my guard for a minute, that I started to feel, deep in my throat, a kind of crying I had never tasted before. It was a cry of grief, of terrible loss, and I knew it was about to rattle me uncontrollably.

Suddenly Dovaleh walked in. He saw me and froze. He took a few uncertain, almost faltering steps to his bed and dug through his backpack. I fell on my bag and rummaged in it and buried my face in it. The big sob dried up at once. After a minute or two, when I didn't hear anything, I thought he'd left and I looked up. He was standing next to his bed with his face to me and his arms at his sides. We exchanged dark, blunted looks. His lips moved; perhaps he wanted to say something. Or perhaps he was trying to smile, so I would remember him, remember us. I must have responded with a sign of warning, or aversion, or disgust. His face twisted and trembled.

And that was all. When I looked up again, it was to see him walking away from the tent.

"And then, on the third day," he shouts, "or maybe the fourth, who can remember? Who the hell can remember anything at all? My memory, of blessed memory . . . Anyway, we're sitting on the ground in a circle and the sun's beating down on us like a bitch. If there's any shade at all, it's only from the vultures waiting for us to drop dead already. The cross-eyed counselor is talking about camouflage or something, when suddenly a woman soldier runs out of the base commander's barracks, she was a sergeant I think, and she gallops over to us, *boom-boom-boom*, a petite woman but with considerable heft, if you know what I mean, busting out of her uniform, legs like a doe, each one a whole doe—heh-heh—and a second later she's at our circle, the drill cadet doesn't even have time to say 'Attention!' and she barks, all out of breath: 'Greenstein, Dov! Is he in this platoon?' "

I remember the scene. Not the soldier herself, but the way she sharply called out his name, which shocked me out of my daydream. His name sailed over me so unexpectedly that I almost jumped up in a panic and said it was me.

"Right then and there I could feel something rotten coming on. And all the kids in my class, my close friends, they all point at me and yell: 'It's him!' Like they're telling her: 'That one! Take him, not me!' With friends like that . . . right?" He laughs and avoids looking at me. "They wouldn't have been much fun at a *selektzia*, you know? So the soldier girl says: 'Come with me to the commander immediately.' And this castrated voice comes out of my mouth: 'But ma'am, Sergeant, what did I do?' My friends think that's hilarious: *'But ma'am, Sergeant, what did I do?'* they all mimic me. Then they start shouting: 'Are you gonna reprimand him for jacking off? Or for stinking up the tent?' They rat me out with all kinds of lies, then they chant: 'Throw Eraser in the slammer! Throw Eraser in the slammer!' Yep, Eraser was another one of my nicknames. Why? I'm glad you asked! Because back then I had freckles, I don't have them anymore, they faded, but I had loads of them—yes, that is correct, *someone shat on the fan,* thank you so much for the original explanation, table nineteen."

He turns his head slowly in the direction of the heckler, his regular gimmick, and glares at him with blank eyes. The club manager aims a spotlight on a thick-fleshed man with a shaved head wearing a yellow jacket. Dovaleh does not remove his gaze. His eyes are open just a slit. The audience bellows.

"Well, good evening, Mr. Tony Soprano decked out in lemon meringue!" he says sweetly. "Welcome to our humble abode, and may you have a very crystal *Nacht.* I understand you're in between medications at the moment, and just my luck, you had to choose this particular evening to get out for some fresh air!" The man's wife laughs and pats his back, and he blows air loudly and shakes off her comforting hand. "It's okay, brother, it's all good, we're just having fun with you. Yoav, give the gentleman a shot of vodka, on me, and don't forget to slip in a couple of Xanax and some Ritalin . . . No, no, you're all right, my man, at the end of the evening you'll be awarded the Al-Qaeda Prize for emotional intelligence. I'm not laughing *at* you, brother, I'm laughing *with* you, okay? Just imagine that I've heard that joke about the fan a couple of thousand times before. We had one kid in class, you and him would have gotten on like a house on fire, he was just like you—spitting image." He puts his hand around his mouth and whispers to us: "All the subtlety of a wrecking ball and the grace of a jockstrap—I'm kidding, sit down! It's a joke! And every time that kid saw me, but every single time, for eight fucking years, he would ask if I wanted an eraser for the freckles. So that's how the name Eraser stuck, see? There don't happen to be any of my old classmates here tonight, do there? No? So I can keep on lying unchecked? Wonderful! Anyhoo, I get up and shake the sand off my ass—by the way, that was how the original Desert Storm started—and I walk away from my posse and follow her, and I know this is it, I'm done for. Right that second I had the feeling I wouldn't be going back anymore. That this whole thing was over for me. My childhood, I mean."

He takes a sip from the flask. The club echoes with that indistinct but irritable pulsing. People are still waiting to see how the evening is going to develop, but his credit is running out. I sense their response in my body like rapidly dropping blood sugar. I remember: a moment before he answered the soldier and stood up, he sought me out and gave me a long, pleading look. I avoided his eyes.

"Talking about childhood," he murmurs, "I was thinking, you know how everyone's all up in arms about bullying these days? Well, I say, some kids just deserve to get bullied. Because if they don't get the crap bullied out of them when they're young, it'll just get worse the older they get, you know what I mean?

"Not funny? Oh, I see. Sophisticated audience, you guys are, with European standards. Okay, no problem, we'll come at it another way, which I think might be more up your alley. Here's a little psychological analysis plus emotional insight. Me, when I was a kid, I had the most accurate scientific gauge for knowing who was popular and who wasn't. I call it the Shoelace Gauge. Let me explain. Let's say a group of kids is walking home from school. Walking, talking, yakking, yelling. You know—kids. One of them crouches down to tie his shoelace. Now, if the group stops right away—but I mean every single one of them, even kids who were looking the other way and didn't see him crouch down—if they all stop where they are and wait for him, then he's in, he's good, he's popular. But if no one even notices him, and only sometime toward the end of senior year, like at graduation, someone goes, 'Hey, anyone know what happened to that dude who stopped to tie his shoelace?' Well, then you know that *that* dude—he's me."

The little woman is perched on the edge of her seat, mouth open slightly, feet pressed tightly together. He gives her a glance while he takes a sip from his flask, then looks into my eyes, a long, deep look. For the first time since he started telling the story, he looks straight at me, and I have a peculiar sense that he's taken an ember from the woman and passed it to me.

"Long story short, I follow the soldier girl, and I get it into my head that either they're going to punish me for something I did—but what could I have done? Me? The biggest klutz in the class, the biggest dork, the biggest sucker? *A good boy* . . ." He winks at the little woman and immediately looks for me. "Wait a minute, Judge, is that even a word anymore? Is that still on the market, 'sucker'? It's not a collector's item?"

There is no hostility in his voice or in his eyes, which confuses me. I confirm that the word is still in currency. He repeats it to himself quietly several times, and I get sucked into whispering it along with him.

"Either that, or it's something to do with my father. He got some bee in his bonnet, maybe decided something about this whole Gadna doesn't sit right with him, it's an affront to his dignity, or maybe he found out that Gadna has something to do with the Labor Party, and he's a Beitar guy, or, most likely of all, he found the dirty magazines I hid behind the window blinds in my room and he's summoned me for consultations. Could be anything. With him, you never really knew where the next punch was going to come from."

He stands at the edge of the stage, very close to the front row of tables, and shoves his hands into his armpits. Some of the people look up at him. Others sink into themselves with an odd, feeble gaze, as though they've given up following him and yet cannot look away.

"And then I realize she's talking to me, the sergeant. She's walking quickly and saying I have to go home right now, there's no time, I have to get to the funeral by four. She doesn't turn her head back to me, like, I don't know, she's afraid to look at me, and don't forget that all this time right in front of my eyes is her ass, which is quite the sight. Truth is, asses are generally a stimulating topic. You tell me, guys, hands to your hearts— I said to *hearts,* table thirteen! Between you and me, have you ever seen a woman who is satisfied with her ass? Even one single woman under the sun?"

He keeps talking. I see his lips move. He waves his hands, he grins. A white, milky fog begins to spread through my head.

"You know that thing where she stands in front of the mirror and looks back from this side, then from the other side—and by the way, when they're talking about their own personal asses, women can rotate their heads three hundred sixty-five degrees, no problem, guaranteed! It's scientific! It's a rotation that only two other organisms in all of nature can perform: sunflowers and crankshafts. And then she turns around like this—"

He demonstrates, almost slipping backward onto the tables. I look around. I see lots of holes. Little sinkholes opening wide to laugh.

"She looks . . . she checks . . . And don't forget she has this app in her head, Google Ass, which at any given moment compares her ass to the size it was when she was seventeen. And very gradually she gets this face, and it's the face she only has in this one particular circumstance, in Latin it's called an endemic face, or in English: ass-face. And then, like a queen in a Greek tragedy, she pronounces: 'That's it. It's starting to fall.' No! It's worse! It's *dropping*. You get that? She starts to sound like her ass's social worker! Like the ass, of its own free will and with premeditated intention, is dropping out, retreating from society, turning its back on civilization, turning into a fringe ass. Any second now you'll find it shooting up in the alleyway. And you, my fellow males, if you happen to be with her in the room at this particular moment, your best course of action is to zip it. Don't say a word! Anything you say can and will be used against you. If you tell her she's exaggerating, that it's actually cute and attractive and pinchable and strokeable—you're done for: you're blind, you're a flatterer, you're an idiot, you don't know the first thing about women. On the other hand, if you tell her she's right—you're a dead man."

He pants. The bit is over. Who knows how many times he's done it before. His voice no longer fills out every word—some of the syllables he swallows. The crowd laughs. I still hope I misheard, that I missed something, that there was a joke that got past me. But when I look at the little medium, her face twisted in pain, I know.

"Where were we? You're such a lovely audience! Honestly, I'd like to take you home with me. Okay, so the ass is walking ahead of me, she's in front and I'm in back, I have no clue what she wants from me, what all that babbling about a funeral was, and I've never even been to a funeral, haven't had the opportunity, I come from a small family, as you know, we've covered that, mom and dad and kid, and we never had funerals, there weren't any relatives left to die—it was just him and her. Wait, that reminds me of something. Since we're on the topic of relatives, I read in the paper this week that scientists discovered that the closest creature to human beings, genetically, is some kind of blind worm that's totally primitive. I swear! This worm and us, we're like this! But I'm starting to think we might be the black sheep of the family, because, otherwise, explain to me why they never invite us to their parties?" He throws another left hook in the air. There is a heavy silence in the room. I believe what he said before is starting to sink in.

"Okay, I get it, I see. Recalculating route. Where were we? Mom-dad-kid. No family. No relatives. We said that. Quiet and calm like the Bermuda Triangle. Yeah, there were a few things here and there, not that you really give that stuff any thought at that age, but I did have some awareness that my father was no spring chicken, and that actually he was the oldest of all the class dads, and I knew he had blood sugar, and heart, and kidneys, and he took pills, and I also knew, well, actually I could see, everyone could see, that his blood pressure was so high he was in a constant state of . . . I don't know . . . Archie Bunker bickering with Edith. And Mom, too, even though she was much younger than him, she had all kinds of baggage from *there* that she carried around. I mean, she spent almost six months shut up in this tiny little compartment in a train car, like a closet for storing paint and grease where you couldn't even stand or sit, it was good times, and apart from all that she also had on her wrist, on both wrists"—he holds his thin forearms up—"these delicate little stitches, the finest vein embroidery, which the top-rated needleworkers gave her at Bikur Holim Hospital. It's interesting, actually, that we both had postpartum depression after I was born, except that with me it's been going on for fifty-seven years. But apart from those little issues, which I'm sure every normal family has, the three of us were pretty much fine, and so what was this business about a funeral?"

The audience, which has been increasingly subdued for the

past few minutes, is now completely still. The faces are devoid of expression. Wary of committing. Maybe that's how I look from the stage, too.

"Where were we? No, don't tell me! Me do it on my own! You know what the opposite of forgetting is at my age?"

A few feeble voices: "Remembering?"

"No: writing down. Okay, so soldier, officer, ass, train, embroidery . . . Right, so I'm behind her, walking slowly, getting even slower, wondering what it could be, it must be a mistake, why would they send *me* to a funeral? Why didn't they pick some other kid?"

He talks fast, holding back an outburst. His hands dig deeper and deeper into his armpits. I think he's trembling a little.

"So I walk and I chew over the thoughts slowly, then even more slowly, and I don't get it, I just don't get it, and all of a sudden I flip over and turn upside down and walk on my hands. I walk behind her, the sand's hot as hell, it burns my hands, doesn't matter, burning is good, burning is not thinking, things fall out of my pocket, change, phone tokens, gum, stuff Dad shoved in there for the road, little surprises, he always did that, especially after he hit me, never mind. I walk quickly, I run"—he holds his hands up over his head and walks them through the air, and I can see they really are shaking, the fingers trembling—"who's gonna find me when I'm upside down? How can anyone catch me?"

Deathly silence. It seems to me that people are trying to understand how—with what sleight of hand, through what trickery or magic—they've been transported from the place they were in a few moments ago to this new story.

I feel the same way. Like the ground is dropping away from under my feet.

"And this girl, the soldier, she suddenly sensed something, maybe she saw my shadow upside down on the ground, and she turned around, I saw her shadow spinning. 'Are you out of your mind?' she yelled, but she was sort of yelling quietly. 'Cadet, back on your feet this instant! Are you mad? Playing around at a time like this?' But me? I just run around next to her, in front of her, behind her, my hands burn, they get pricked by thorns, stones, gravel, but I don't flip back up. What's she going to do to me? You can't do anything to me when I'm like that, and there's no thoughts that way, my head is full of blood, ears plugged, no brain, no one to think, no *What the hell she's not allowed to yell at me,* no *What does she mean 'at a time like this'?*"

He walks very slowly, his hands still up in the air, step after step after step, and the tip of his tongue sticks out between his lips. The big copper urn behind him traps his body, sucks it into its curves, and divides it into waves until he extricates himself.

"And by the way, I can see my pals, too, upside down, sitting right where I left them, listening to the instructor, learning about camouflage, which is a good skill to have in life, not even turning their heads to see what's up with me—remember the Shoelace Gauge? I see them getting farther and farther away, and I know it's me getting farther away, but bottom line: me and them are far apart."

Liora, the girl from my class who was on guard duty with me at the north post the night before, I had loved passionately for almost two years and had never had the guts to talk to. Dovaleh knew I was in love with her. He was the only one in the world I'd told about her. The only one who knew to ask me about her, and to really extract from me, with his piercing Socratic questions, the understanding that I loved her. That this emotion that tortured me in her presence—and made me even more gloomy and aggressive—was love. When we were on guard duty together that night, at 3:00 a.m., I kissed Liora. I touched a girl's body for the first time. My years of loneliness were over, and, one could say, my new life had begun.

And he was with me there. I mean, I talked to her the way I talked with him. The way he taught me in our walkie-talkie conversations. And I had learned well: as soon as we got to the guard post, I asked her about her parents, and where they'd met, and then about her two brothers. She was amazed. It knocked her off-balance. I needled her patiently but stubbornly, and slyly, until she gradually told me about her older brother, who was autistic and lived in an institution and was almost never spoken of at home. I had been a star pupil and I was prepared for the encounter: I knew how to ask and I knew how to listen. Liora talked and cried, and talked and cried some more, and when I made her laugh she laughed through her tears, and I stroked her and hugged her and kissed her tears away. There was a spuriousness on my part that, to this day, I have trouble understanding completely. Some sort of skeleton-key trickery. I felt that I was aiming myself to the Dovaleh I knew, the beloved old Dovaleh. I was reviving him from inside myself for the benefit of this moment with Liora, letting his words flow out of my throat. And I was levelheaded enough to know that afterward I would once again erase him.

That morning, when I sat on the sandy quad with my platoon and the sergeant came for him, I was drunk. Drunk on love and a sense of redemption and lack of sleep. I saw him get up and follow her, and I didn't even wonder where he was going. Then I must have sunk back into fantasizing about Liora and the unbelievably soft texture of her lips and her breasts and the tufts of down in her armpits, and when I looked again I saw him walking behind the sergeant on his hands. I'd never seen him do that before and it had never occurred to me that he was capable of it. He walked fast, light, and because of the intense heat that roiled the air, his body seemed to radiate ripples. It was a wondrous spectacle. He suddenly looked free and cheerful, prancing on waves of air as if he were defeating the laws of gravity and becoming his own self again. My affection for him washed over me, and the torture of the last few days was wiped away.

For one moment.

But I couldn't tolerate it. Him. His ups and downs. I looked away from him. I remember the movement clearly. And I sank back into my new intoxication.

"So we keep running, her upright and me the other way, with thistles and sand and signs running in front of my eyes, and we get to the path with white stones that leads to the commander's barracks, and I can hear yelling from inside: 'You're taking him right now!' 'Fuck if I'm going all the way there!' 'You get him to the funeral by four, that's an order!' 'I've been back and forth to Jerusalem three times already this week!' Then I hear someone else, and I recognize the voice immediately: it's the drill sergeant, the one we called Eichmann—that was the nickname of choice back then for the compassionately challenged—and he's yelling, too, and his voice is louder than all the others: *'But where the hell is he? Where's the orphan kid?'*"

He grins apologetically. His arms hang beside his body.

I stare at the table. At my hands. I didn't know.

"My hands turn to butter. I fall over and lie with my head on the ground. And I lie there and lie there for I don't know how long. And when I manage to lift my head, I see that I'm alone. Are you getting the picture? Yours truly splattered all over the desert sand, the sergeant chick is long gone, she took off, that chubby cheeks, that sweet little mitzvah tank, I guarantee you that girl did not have a poster of Oskar Schindler hanging over her bed."

I didn't know. It never occurred to me. How could I have known?

"Come on now, Netanya honey, stay with me. I need you to hold my hand. So in front of me are these kind of wooden steps leading up to the commander's barracks, above me blazing sun and eagles, all around me seven bloodthirsty Arab states, and inside they're yelling at each other like madmen: 'I'm only taking him as far as Be'er Sheva! Someone from the command will have to take him from there to Jerusalem!' 'Okay, okay, you dumbass, I heard you, just take the kid already and go, we don't have time for this. *Go*, I'm telling you!'"

People straighten up a little in their seats and start breathing again, carefully. The story is rousing them now, together with the narrator's newfound energy, and his gesticulations, the impersonations, the accents.

Dovaleh, onstage, can feel the new spirit immediately, and he looks around with a grin. Each smile births another and they pop out like soap bubbles.

"So I pick myself up from the sand and I wait, and the door opens, and a pair of red shoes stuffed with drill sergeant walks down the steps, and he goes: 'Let's go, buddy. My condolences.' And he holds his hand out for a shake. *Yikes—the drill sergeant is shaking my hand!* He kind of snivels, like that's his way of signaling muffled-sadness-slash-grief: 'Sergeant Ruchama told you already, right? Sorry, buddy, this can't be easy. Especially at your age. Just know you're in good hands, we'll get you there like clockwork, but we gotta run and grab your stuff now.'

"That's what the drill sergeant says, and me"—he opens his eyes wide in a terrifying dollish expression—"I'm in total shock, I'm not taking in anything, all I get is that I'm not going to be punished for anything, and I'm also realizing this is not the same douche-bag drill sergeant who's been busting our balls all week. No, now he's all fatherly: 'Come with me, buddy, the ride's waiting, buddy.' Any minute he'd have said, 'Thank you for choosing us, buddy, we know you had the choice of losing a parent on many other army bases . . .'

"Okay, so off we go, me dragging like a doormat behind all six foot six of his dense matter, and you know how drill sergeants walk, like cyborgs—head up, legs as far apart as they can get 'em so people will think they must be hung like a horse down there, fists clenched, pecs flapping right to left with every step." He demonstrates. "Drill sergeants, you know, they don't walk—they *spell out* the walk, isn't that right? Was anyone here a drill sergeant in the army? No way, man! What unit? Golani? Wait, are there any paratroopers here? Awesome! Let's go, guys, duke it out!" The crowd laughs. The two gray-haired men hold their glasses up to each other from afar.

"By the way, Golani, d'you know how a Golanchik commits suicide?"

The guy shouts back: "Jumps off his ego onto his IQ!"

"Bravo, sir!" Dovaleh cheers. "Now would you mind not stealing my job?

"Bottom line, we get to the tent and the drill sergeant stands aside—as in, to give me some privacy. I shove everything my dad packed for me into my backpack. In case you haven't figured it out yet, I was a mama's boy but a papa's soldier, and my dad pimped my gear out so I had everything a proper commando might need when he sets off for Operation Entebbe. Mom wanted to help, too, and she had a lot of experience with camping, as we've mentioned—although her camps were more of the concentration variety. Anyhoo, by the time the two of them had finished packing for me, I was equipped for any possible development on the international or regional front, including asteroid-induced jock itch."

He stops, smiles at some recollection that pops into his mind, perhaps the picture of his father and mother packing. He slaps his thigh and laughs. He laughs! An ordinary laugh, from inside, not the professional kind. Not the toxic, self-deprecating snicker. Just a person laughing. A few people quickly join in, as do I—how can I resist wading in with him for a moment of tenderness toward himself?

"Seriously, you should have seen her and my dad's packing show. Better than any stand-up routine. You'd have asked yourself: Who are these two weirdos and who's the Einstein who invented them and why the hell can't I get a brilliant mind like that to come work for me? And then you'd think: Oh, shit! He *does* work for me! Picture this: My dad comes in, goes out, runs back in, hurries out. The way he moved—you know those little flies that only go in straight lines? *Bzzz bzzz!* He keeps coming back from their bedroom with one more thing, puts it in the bag, arranges everything, packs it in, runs out for something else, towel, flashlight, mess kit, *bzzz*, cookies, *bzzz*, bouillon cubes, first-aid cream, hats, inhaler, talcum powder, socks . . . Crams it all in, tamps it into a perfect cube, doesn't even see me, I don't exist for him, it's just him against the backpack, all-out war, toothpaste, bug repellent, that plastic thing for your nose so it doesn't get sunburned, *bzzz,* runs out, runs back in, his eyes get even closer to each other . . .

"I'm telling you, he was unparalleled at these things: organizing, planning, taking care of me. He was a pro, he was in his element. Do you even understand how stressful it is when you're three and your dad makes you take a different route to preschool every day to confuse the enemy?"

Laughter.

"No, seriously, when I was in first grade the guy used to stand outside my classroom interrogating the other kids: 'Is that your bag? Did you pack it yourself? Did anyone give you anything to deliver?'"

Hearty laughter.

"Then my mom turns up with a big wool coat, I don't know whose it was, it reeked of mothballs. Why the coat, Mom? 'Cause she'd heard it was cold at night in the desert. So he takes it from her very gently, like this, and goes, '*Nu, Saraleh, yetz ist zimmer, di nar zitz unt kik,*' which means 'It's summer now, you just sit and watch.' Like hell she'd sit and watch! A second later she's back with boots. Why? Because! Because after you've walked barefoot through snow for more than thirty miles, you don't leave home without them." He waves his ridiculous boots at us. "You have to understand, this woman had never seen a desert in her life. From the second she got to Israel she only left home to go to work, and she had a regular route like a cuckoo in its clock, apart from that episode where she went all Goldilocks on the estates around Rehavia, but we won't go into that. And always with her head down and the *schmatte* over her face so no one could see her, God forbid, chop-chop alongside the walls and fences so no one would snitch on her to God and He'd find out she existed."

He stops for a sip. He wipes his glasses on the hem of his shirt, stealing a few seconds of respite. My tapas finally arrive. I've ordered far too much, enough for two. I ignore the looks. I know this is no time for a feast, but I have to steady my blood sugar, so I scarf down the empanadas and grilled mullet and ceviche and pickled mushrooms. Turns out that once again I ordered the dishes *she* likes, which will undoubtedly give me heartburn. She laughs: *Well, if this is the only way, it'll have to count as a kind of meeting.* I wolf everything down and turn bilious. It's not enough, I tell her with my mouth full. *This make-believe game we play is not enough for me; I'm not satisfied with one-player ping-pong, or with having to sit here on my own with his story. You and your new boyfriend . . .* I almost choke, and the wasabi prickles my nose and brings tears to my eyes. She quickly turns her impish smirk into a million-dollar smile and coquettishly responds: *Don't say that! Death isn't my boyfriend yet. We're just friends. Maybe friends with benefits.*

"Where were we?" he mumbles. "What was I saying? Oh, right, my mother. She couldn't do anything. None of the homemaking things, the mom things," he grumbles, veering off onto an internal detour. "Couldn't do laundry, couldn't iron, definitely couldn't cook. I don't even think she made an egg her whole life. But my dad did things no other man does. You should have seen the way he kept the towels neatly folded and stacked in the linen cupboard, and the drapes with perfect pleats, and the polished floor." He wrinkles his forehead and his eyebrows actually collide. "He even ironed our underwear, for all three of us. I'll tell you something that'll make you laugh—"

"It's about time!" a short, broad-shouldered man shouts. A few more voices join in: "Where are the jokes? What's going on here? What is this crap?"

"One sec, bro, I've got a new shipment coming in any minute, you'll like this, I guarantee it! I just wanted to . . . What was I . . . I'm all confused now, you got me off course. Listen, dude, listen to me closely, you've never heard anything like this. My father, he had an arrangement with a shoe shop on Yafo—you know Yafo Street in Jerusalem? Bravo, you citizen of the world, you! So this place had him mend stockings for women in Me'a She'arim and those other neighborhoods. It was another one of Captain Longstocking's start-ups, another way to make a few shekels on the side. I'm telling you, that man could've sold shoes to a fish!"

Feeble laughter. Dovaleh wipes the sweat off his brow with the back of his hand. "Listen closely now. He used to bring stockings home every week to mend, piles of them, forty, fifty pairs each time, and he taught her how to darn them, that was another of his skills, he could fix ladders in nylons, can you believe it?"

He's talking only to the short, broad-shouldered man now. With one hand he makes a pleading, supplicating gesture: Wait a sec, bro, you'll get your joke hot out of the oven any minute now, it's almost done. "He bought her a special needle with a little wooden handle thingy . . . Oh, man, it's all coming back to me now, you brought it all back to me, I love you, you're my hero! So she'd put the stocking over one hand, and she'd darn eye after eye in the ladder with that needle until there was no ladder left, and she'd do this for hours, sometimes all night, eye after eye—"

He's hardly paused for a breath these last few minutes, racing to get to the finish line before the audience's patience runs out. The room is quiet. Here and there a woman smiles, perhaps at a distant memory of those old-fashioned nylons. But no one laughs.

"Look how it's all coming back . . . ," he murmurs apologetically.

A man's voice grunts through the silence: "Listen, buddy, bottom line—are we gonna get any comedy here tonight or not?"

It's the man with the shaved head and the yellow jacket. I had a feeling he'd be back. The other man, the one with the massive shoulder span, backs him up with a grunt. A couple of supportive voices chime in. A few others, mostly women, try to shush them, and the man in yellow says: "Seriously, people, we came for some laughs and this guy's giving us a Holocaust memorial day. And he's making *jokes* about the Holocaust!"

"You are absolutely right, my friend, and I do apologize. I'm gonna make it right for you. Now what was I thinking . . . Oh yeah, I have to tell you this one! A guy visits his grandma's grave on the anniversary of her death. A few rows away he sees a man sitting next to a grave crying, shouting, 'Why? *Why?* Why did you have to die? Why were you taken from me? What is my life worth now that you're gone? O cursed death!' Well, after a few minutes the grandson can't resist and he goes over to the guy: 'Excuse me for disturbing you, sir, but I'm really touched by your expression of sorrow. I've never seen such profound grief. Could I ask whom you are mourning? Was it your son? Your brother?' The guy looks at him and goes, 'Of course not—it's my wife's first husband.'"

Big laughs—decidedly exaggerated considering the joke— and here and there some forced applause. It's heart-wrenching to see how eager people are to help him salvage the evening.

"But wait, there's more! I've got enough stock to last till

midnight!" he shrieks, and his eyes dart around. "Guy calls up someone who went to high school with him thirty years ago and says, 'I have tickets for the cup final tomorrow, wanna go?' The other guy's surprised, but a free ticket doesn't come along every day, so he says yes. They get to the match, they sit down, great seats, awesome atmosphere, they have fun, they yell, they curse, they do the wave, see some great moves. At halftime the friend says, 'Listen, dude, I have to ask—didn't you have anyone closer than me, like a relative, to give the ticket to?' Other dude says, 'No.' 'And you didn't want to bring, I don't know, your wife?' 'My wife's dead,' he says. Guy from high school goes, 'Oh, I'm sorry to hear that. Then what about one of your closer friends? Or someone from work?' 'Believe me, I tried,' the guy says, 'but they all said they'd rather go to her funeral.'"

The crowd laughs. Cheers fly over to the stage, but the guy with the big shoulders cups his hands over his mouth and booms: "Ixnay on the funerals already! Give us some life!" This rakes in quite a few cheers and claps, and as Dovaleh looks at the audience I can feel that for the past few minutes, even with all the jokes and the fireworks, he's been absent. He is turning more and more inward, and he seems to be slowing down, and that's not good, he could lose the crowd. He could lose the whole evening. And there's no one to protect him.

"No more funerals. Got it, bro. You make a good point. I'm taking notes, learning on the job. Listen, Netanya, let's lighten things up, yeah? But I still have to tell you something a little bit personal, some might say intimate, because I feel like we've really clicked. Yoav, can you just turn up the air? We can't breathe in here!"

The audience claps enthusiastically.

"So here's the deal. I was walking around town here before

the show, checking out escape routes, like in case you decided to kick me off the stage"—he chuckles, but a weight hangs at the edge of the laugh, and everyone knows it—"and all of a sudden I see an old guy, maybe eighty, all dried up like a raisin, sitting on a street bench crying. An old man crying? How can I not go over? He might be in a will-changing mood. I walk up to him softly and ask, 'Sir, why are you crying?' 'What else can I do?' the old man answers. 'A month ago, I met a thirty-year-old woman. She's beautiful, adorable, sexy, and we fell in love and moved in together.' 'That's awesome!' I say. 'So what's the problem?' Old guy says, 'I'll tell you. We start every day with two hours of wild sex, then she makes me some pomegranate juice for the iron, and I go to the doctor's office. I come back, we have more wild sex, and she makes me a spinach quiche for the antioxidants. In the afternoon I play cards with the guys at the club, I come home, we have wild sex into the night, and this is how it goes, day after day . . . ' 'Sounds fantastic!' I tell him. 'I'd like me some of that! But then why are you crying?' Old guy thinks for a minute and says, 'I can't remember where I live.'"

The crowd erupts. He gauges it like a hiker testing the steadiness of a river rock, and even before the last cheers die down, he charges ahead: "Where were we? Drill sergeant . . . Cyborg . . ." He mimics the stiff gait again and flashes an ingratiating smile that knots up my stomach. "So the drill sergeant's breathing down my neck: 'Let's go, gotta hurry, we can't have you being late, God forbid, you can't miss it.' And I go, 'Miss what, sir?' And he looks at me like I'm retarded. 'They're not going to wait all day for you,' he says, 'you know what funerals are like, especially in Jerusalem with all their religious laws. Didn't Ruchama tell you you have to be at Givat Shaul at four?' 'Who's Ruchama?' I sit on my cot staring at the sergeant. And I swear to you, I've never seen a drill sergeant from up close like that, except maybe in *National Geographic* magazine. And he says, 'They called from your school to inform you, the principal himself called and said you have to be at the cemetery at four.' And I still don't understand what he's telling me. All these words they keep saying to me, it's like I'm hearing them for the first time in my life. Why would the principal be talking about me? How does he even know who I am? What exactly did he say? And there's another question I need to ask, but I'm too embarrassed, I don't know how you ask something like that, especially when it's the drill sergeant, a guy I really don't know. So what comes out instead is that I ask why I have to pack my bag. He looks up at the tent roof like he's totally given up on me. 'Kiddo,' he says, 'don't you get it yet? You're not coming back here.' I ask why. 'Because the shiva,' he says, 'will only be over after your pals are done here.'

"Oh, great, so now the plan includes sitting shiva, too? They really thought of everything, didn't they? Except they forgot to let me in on the plans. And while I'm listening to this information, all I can think is that I'm dying to sleep. Yawning all the time. Right in the sergeant's face. I can't control it. I clear some room for myself on the bed among all the stuff and I lie down and close my eyes and wipe out."

He shuts his eyes and stands there motionless. With his eyes closed, oddly, his face looks more lucid and expressive, somehow more spiritual even. He fingers the hem of his shirt absentmindedly. My heart goes out to him, until he opens his mouth:

"You know those army cots, the ones that fold in on you in the middle of the night and swallow you up like a carnivorous plant? Your friends turn up in the morning and there's no Dovaleh, no nothing, just your glasses and maybe a shoelace, and the bed is licking its lips and belching?"

A few giggles here and there. The audience isn't sure it's allowed to laugh at such a time. Only the two kids in leather give a long but soft belly laugh, a strange purr that scatters disquiet around the tables nearby. I look at them and think about how for twenty years, every single day, I soaked up radiation from people like them, until there came a moment, after Tamara, without Tamara, when I guess I couldn't take it anymore and I started spewing it back out.

"Drill sergeant goes, 'Get up! What the hell are you doing lying down?' So I get up and wait. Like the second he leaves, I'm going back to sleep. Not for long, just until it all passes and we forget the whole thing and go back to the way it was before all this crap.

"And now he's getting annoyed at me, but carefully annoyed. 'Move,' he goes, 'stand here, let me pack up your stuff.' I don't get it. The sergeant is going to pack my stuff for me? That's like . . . I don't know . . . like Saddam Hussein comes up to you in a restaurant and says, 'Might I interest you in some caramelized forest-berry soufflé I just whipped up?'"

He stops and waits for a response that is slow to come. He quickly diagnoses the audience's quagmire: his story has annihilated the possibility of laughter. I can see how his thought process works. He quickly redraws the playing field, gives us permission: "Did you hear the one about the woman with a terminal illness, the name of which shall go unmentioned so as not to give it any subliminal advertising?" He cheerfully opens his arms for a big hug. "Anyway, the woman says to her husband, 'I dreamed that if we have anal sex, I'll get better.' You don't know this one? Are you living under a rock? Okay, listen. So the husband, he thinks this sounds a little weird, but a guy'll do anything to make his wife better, right? So they get into bed that night, they do it doggy-style, and they fall asleep. In the morning the husband wakes up, reaches out to her side of the bed—it's empty! He jumps up, convinced this is the end, but then he hears her singing in the kitchen. He runs in and finds his wife standing there making a salad, all smiles. She looks fantastic. 'You won't believe this,' she says, 'I slept great, woke up early, felt incredible, so I went to the hospital, they ran some tests, did a couple of X-rays, and they said I'm cured! I'm a medical miracle!' The husband hears this and bursts into tears. 'Why are you crying?' she asks. 'Aren't you happy I'm better?' 'Of course I am,' he says, sobbing, 'but I can't help thinking I could have saved Mom, too!' "

Some turn up their noses, but most like it. I do, too. It's a good joke, there's no getting around it. I hope I'll be able to remember it. Dovaleh does a quick scan. "Good move," he tells himself out loud, "you still have it after all, Dovi." He pats his chest with his fingers spread wide, a gesture only slightly different from the earlier blows.

"So I stand up and the sergeant attacks my backpack. He picks up all the crap that's scattered on the bed, and under the bed, he charges in like he's storming a house in the occupied territories. *Bam!* Shoves it all in, crams the bag full without any order, no form, no thought, what's Dad going to say when I come home with the backpack in this state? And the minute I think about that, my knees buckle and I fall onto a different cot."

He shrugs his shoulders. Smiles weakly. I think he's having trouble breathing.

"Okay, let's get this show on the road, mustn't irritate the audience, we're instant-gratification kind of people, chop-chop! So I pick up the backpack and run after the drill sergeant, and from the corner of my eye I can see my friends on the quad looking at me like they already know something, like maybe they saw the eagles flying north: *Amigos!*" He acts out the eagles' cries in a heavy Russian accent. *"There's fresh blood in Jerusalem!"*

I saw him follow the drill sergeant, his small body hunched under the weight of the backpack. I remember that we all turned to look at him, and it occurred to me that apart from the backpack he looked just the way he did when we said good-bye at the bus stop and he dragged himself begrudgingly to his neighborhood.

One of his classmates threw out some joke about him, but this time nobody laughed. We didn't know why they'd come to take him to the commander, and I don't know if by the time we finished the camp any of his classmates had found out what had happened or where they'd taken him. None of the command-ers told us anything, and we didn't ask. Or at least I didn't. All I knew was that a soldier had come to get him, he'd gotten up and followed her, and a few minutes later I'd seen him trail the drill sergeant all the way to a waiting pickup truck. Those were the facts before me that day. The next time I saw him was when he walked onstage this evening.

"And the driver's going pedal to the metal in neutral, all his pissed-off energy is concentrated in his foot, and he looks at me like he wants to kill me. I climb up, toss my bag in the back, and sit in the front next to him, and the drill sergeant says to him: 'You see this nice boy? You're not letting go of his hand until you get him to the Central Bus Station in Be'er Sheva and some-one from HQ comes to take him from your hand to Jerusalem.

Capeesh?' And the driver goes: 'I swear on the Bible, Sarge, if they're not there when I get there, I'm leaving him at lost and found.' The sergeant pinches the driver's cheek hard and grins right in his face: 'Listen, Tripoli, don't forget what I have on you, eh? You leave this kid there—I'll leave my foot in your ass. If you don't deliver him personally into the palm of their hand, that's an unreturned equipment rap for you. Now go!'

"And me, just so you understand, all this is like I'm watching a movie with me in it. There I am sitting in an army truck, and there are two people I don't know, both soldiers, talking about me, but in a language I don't fully understand, and there's no closed captions. And I keep wanting to ask the drill sergeant something, I really urgently need to ask him before we go, and I'm just waiting for him to stop talking for a second, but when he stops I can't do it, the words don't come out, they won't join together, I'm scared shitless of them—those two little words.

"Then he looks at me and I think, Okay, now he's going to tell me, here it comes. I'm preparing myself, my whole body slams shut. And he puts his hand on my head like a yarmulke and says, 'May the Almighty comfort you among the mourners of Zion and Jerusalem.' Then he slaps his hand on the side of the pickup the way you slap a horse to make it gallop, and the driver says, 'Amen,' and puts his foot on the gas, and we're off."

The crowd is silent. One woman holds up a hesitant hand like a pupil in class, then puts it back in her lap. At a nearby table a man gives his wife a confused look, and she shrugs her shoulders.

The man in the yellow jacket is approaching his boiling point. Dovaleh senses it and glances at him nervously. I call the waitress to clear my table—immediately. Can't stand to look at these empty little dishes. I can't believe I ate so much.

"So bottom line, we drive. Driver doesn't talk. I don't even know his name. Thin guy, kind of hunched, with a huge nose and giant ears and a face full of acne all the way to his neck. Loads more zits than I have. Neither of us talks. He's got it in for me because they screwed him with this trip, and I'm certainly not saying anything—what can I say? It's over a hundred degrees and I'm drenched in sweat. The driver turns the radio on, but there's no reception, just noise, static, nothing but Martian stations." Here he does a perfect imitation of poorly received stations rapidly switching, a gibberish of sentence fragments and snatches of songs: "Jerusalem of Gold," "Johnny Is the Goy for Me," "*Itbah al-Yahud,*" "I Want to Hold Your Hand," "Even when the cannons roar our desire for peace shall never die!" "I wish they all could be California girls . . ." "Merci stockings—try them today!" "The Temple Mount is in our hands!"

Delighted laughter. Dovaleh drinks from his flask and looks at me as if he's wondering what I think about the story so far, or maybe about the whole show. With a stupid, cowardly reflex, I shut my face off, erase my expression, and look away. He recoils as though I'd struck him.

Why did I do that? Why did I withhold my support at that moment? I wish I knew. I understand so little of myself, and in recent years less and less. When there's no one to talk to, when there's no Tamara probing, insisting, my inner channels get clogged up. I remember how furious she was after she came to court to watch me preside over a case of an abusive father. "You had no expression at all on your face!" she fumed afterward, at home. "The poor girl was pouring her heart out, she looked at you with pleading eyes, just waiting for you to show her a sign, any little sign of support, of understanding, one look to show her that your heart was with her, and you—"

I explained that it was precisely that face that I needed to show in court: even if inside I was exploding, I could not so much as hint at my feelings, because I had not yet made up my mind. And, I explained, that very stone face I gave the girl I later gave her father when he offered his version. "Justice must be visible," I insisted, "and I promise you that all my empathy for the girl will be expressed in my verdict." "But by then," Tamara said, "it'll be too late for what she needed when she talked to you in those horrible moments." And she gave me a look I'd never seen from her before.

"But here's the deal, Netanya," he says, trying to sound cheerful, clearly attempting to get past my offense, and I can barely contain my own anger at myself. "Ah, Netanya!" He sighs. "Halcyon city! I just love sharing things with you. Where were we? Right. The driver. So I'm starting to sense that he's feeling a little bad about how he treated me, and he's trying to get a conversation going. Or maybe he's just bored, and hot, and the flies. But me— what the hell do I have to talk with him about? And also, I don't know if he knows. If they told him about me. If when he was in the room with the commander and the sergeant, they told him. And let's say he does know, right? I still don't know how to ask him. Besides, I'm not even sure I can stand being told, and me all alone to boot, without Mom and Dad—"

Now it bursts out. The shaved-head man in the yellow jacket pounds the table with an open hand, once, twice, slowly, his eyes fixed on Dovaleh and his face expressionless. Within seconds the club ossifies, and the only thing moving is that arm. Pound. Pause. Pound.

An eternity passes.

Very slowly, from the edges of the room, a tentative murmur of protest arises. But he persists: Pound. Pause. Pound. The stubby man with the broad shoulders joins in with his fist clenched, almost cracking the table with his slow punches. The blood rushes to my head. There they are. Those types.

They encourage each other with silent looks. That's all they need. The murmur around them crescendos into a commotion. A few tables support them enthusiastically, some protest, most are wary of expressing any opinion. A thin smell of sweat permeates the air in the basement space. Even the perfumes smell acrid. The club manager stands there helplessly.

Intertable arguments spring up: "But he *is* putting jokes in, all the time!" one woman insists. "I've been keeping track, I'm telling you!" "And anyway, stand-up isn't just about jokes," another woman backs her up, "sometimes it's also funny stories from life." "Okay, I can live with stories, but his stories have no point!" a man my age yells while an artificially tanned woman leans on him.

Dovaleh turns to look at me with his whole body.

At first I don't know what he wants. He stands on the edge of the stage ignoring the tempest, looking at me. He's still hoping I'll do something for him. But what can I do? What can be done against these people?

Then comes the thought of what I used to be able to do; of the powers I had in the face of such people. The authority I could wield with a wave of the hand, with a few words. The regal feeling, which I was forbidden to confess to, even in private.

The noise and shouts escalate. Almost everyone is involved in the commotion now, and there is the gleeful anticipation of a fight in the air. Still he stands there looking at me. He needs me.

It's been a long time since someone needed me. It's hard to describe the magnitude of the surprise that floods me. And the panic. I have a coughing attack, then I push the table away from me, stand up, and still have no idea what I'm going to do. I might simply walk out—what am I even doing in this thuggish place? I should have left an hour ago. But those two are pounding the tables, and there's Dovaleh, and I hear myself shout: "Let him tell his story already!"

Everyone falls silent and looks at me with a mixture of horror and dread, and I realize I've shouted much louder than I meant to.

I stand there. Stuck. Like an actor in a melodrama waiting for someone to whisper his lines. But no one does. And there are no bouncers in this club to separate me from the crowd, no panic button under the table, and this is not the world in which I used to relish walking down the street as a commoner, knowing that in a few moments I would be a fate sealer.

I am breathing too fast but cannot control it. Eyes glare at me. I know my appearance is a little misleading—sometimes the prominent, lumpy forehead does the job just as well as the heft—but I'm not such a hero that I can stand behind my outburst if things really get dicey.

"Let him tell his story," I repeat, this time slowly, emphatically, pressing each word into the air, and I move into a sort of head-butting stance. I know I look ridiculous, but I keep standing there, remembering what it feels like to fill my being to its brink. To be.

The man in yellow turns to look at me. "No problem, Your

Honor, no disrespect, I'm with you, but I would like him to tell me what all this bullshit has to do with the two hundred forty shekels I threw away here this evening. Isn't this some sort of misdemeanor, Your Honor? Aren't you getting a whiff of false advertising?"

Dovaleh, whose eyes are shining at me with the gratitude a boy might feel toward an older brother coming to his defense, leaps in: "It is one hundred percent connected, my friend, it absolutely is! And now is when it gets most connected, I swear. Up to now it was just foreplay, you get me?" He gives the protester an ill-conceived man-to-man grin that makes him look away as though he'd seen an open wound. "Listen carefully, my friend: So I put my head against the window, and it's an army-issue window, which bottom line means you can't close it all the way, but you also can't open it all the way, and the glass is just stuck there in the middle and it shudders, but I'm actually digging that, because it doesn't just shudder, it goes apeshit! *D-d-d-d-d!* Horrible noise, I mean, a jackhammer drilling a fucking brick wall doesn't make that kind of noise, so naturally I put my head on it, and within seconds it starts scrambling my brain—*d-d-d-d-d!* I'm in a blender! An air compressor! *D-d-d-d-d! D-d-d-d-d!*"

He illustrates the way he leaned on the window. His head starts shaking, gently at first, then faster and stronger, until his whole body is convulsing, and it's a wondrous sight: his features blend together, expressions cross over one another in flight like cards in a deck being shuffled. His limbs flutter and dance as he jerks around the stage, tossed from one edge to the other, then he flops onto the floor like a Raggedy Ann and lies there panting, the occasional spasm jolting his arm or leg.

The crowd resumes laughing. Even the rabble-rousers chuckle, almost despite themselves, and the little medium grins.

"I'm telling you, it was a blessing in disguise, that *drrrr,*" he projects. He gets up, dusts his hands off, and smiles heartily at the man in yellow, then at the guy with the shoulders. The two of them are still resistant, with the same dubious mockery on their faces.

"*Drrrr!* Can't think anything, don't feel anything, every thought gets crushed into a thousand pieces, I'm thought-paste, *drrrr!*" He jiggles his shoulders at the little woman and she bounces and guffaws and pearly tears roll down her cheeks. The few people who notice seem to relish the little subplot. "Pitz," he says to her, "I remember you now. Your family lived upstairs from the widow with the cats."

She beams at him: "I told you I *was.*"

"But the driver—he's no sucker!" he yells and stomps his feet and shoots an Elvis arm up: "He's on to the windowpane trick, he's seen it before, other passengers have done the window-Parkinson's act. So he starts talking to me, all casual like, points out other vehicles on the road: 'That's a Dodge D200 on its way to Shivta. That's an REO taking supplies to Bahad One. That's a Studebaker Lark from Southern Command, Moshe Dayan had one in the war. See that? He's flashing his lights at me, he knows me.' But me, what the hell do I have to say about that? Nothing. Zip. So he takes a different tack: 'Did they seriously just come over and tell you, just like that?'

"Nothing from me. *Drrrrr* . . . Thought-blender. Takes me half a sec to pulverize his question into paste, mashed brain. Then suddenly my father jumps up with his lokshen noodles. I have no idea why that picture decided to pop into my mind right then. Just give me a second on this, okay? After all, it's a pretty impressive thing that my father turns up with his lokshen all of a sudden, because why do you think he did that? Maybe it's not a good sign? Maybe it is? What do I know. I shut my eyes tighter, bang my head against the window harder, best thing I can do now is not think, not think about anything or anyone." He grips his head with both hands and his head rocks between them, and he yells at us as if he's trying to drown out the noise from the pickup truck and the rattling window. "This is something I figured out from the very first minute, Netanya. That what I need to do right now is flip the circuit breaker in my brain! It's not good for me to think about him. Not good for my father either, and basically not good for anyone to be inside my brain right now."

He smiles sweetly and opens his arms for another hug. He gets a few confused laughs. I beam at him with every muscle in my face, to fortify him for the road ahead. I don't know if he can see my smile. How inadequate are the expressions our faces offer us.

"Okay, so what's up with the lokshen? I'm glad you asked! You're an amazing crowd, you guys! A caring and sensitive crowd! So listen. You have to hear this. Once a week, after he gets done with the ledgers, he makes noodles for the week's chicken soup. I swear, true story. So all of a sudden in the truck my brain shows me a movie, don't ask me why, brains will be brains, don't expect them to be logical. Here, it's like this, this is how his hands move when he makes the dough, and this is how he rolls it out paper-thin—"

Almost without changing a single note on his face or body, he slides into character. I've never seen his father, only a crude imitation of him that night in the tent at Be'er Ora, but the chill that runs down my spine tells me it's him; that is how he really is.

"And he runs with the dough looped over his arms to hang it on their bed to dry, walks quickly back and forth, zipping around the house, and everything he does he also says it out loud, a running commentary to himself: 'Now take the dough, now put the dough on the *lokshenbrat*, now take the *volgerholtz* and make the dough rolled out.'"

There are some giggles, because of the accent, because of the impersonation, because of the Yiddish, because of Dovaleh's own barreling laughter. But most of the audience sits looking at him without any expression, and I'm beginning to sense that this gaze is the audience's most effective weapon.

"This guy, I swear, the whole time you're at home with him, you hear him talking to himself, giving himself instructions, there's a constant hum coming from him. Honestly, he's a funny guy. Unless he happens to be your father. And now imagine me—me, yeah? You see me? Hello! Wake up! This is your Dovaleh talking! The star of your show! Nice city, Netanya. So I'm like in some crazy movie sitting in the middle of the desert and I suddenly see him right in front of me, my father, like he's right there with all his gestures and his talking, and he takes a knife and cuts the rolled-up dough really fast like a machine, *whack whack whack,* and the lokshen fly out from under the knife, and the knife is a hairsbreadth from his fingers, and he never once gets cut. Cannot happen! My mom, by the way, was not an authorized user of knives in our home." He produces a grin that he stretches as wide as possible, then a little wider. "For example, she was allowed to peel a banana only in the presence of a surgical team. Every single implement would wound her and make her bleed." He winks at us and slowly runs a finger over each forearm, where he had earlier marked what he called her vein embroidery. "And suddenly, what do I see, Netanya?" His face is flushed and sweaty. "What do I see?" He waits for an answer, summoning it with his hand gestures, but no one responds. The crowd is stone cold. "I see her! Mom!" He gives an obsequious snort, aimed mostly at the two exasperated men. "Are you digging me, guys? It's like my brain right away throws pictures of her at me, too—"

The man in the yellow jacket stands up. He slams some money down on the table and yanks his wife up by the arm. Strangely, I feel almost relieved: this is more like it. We're back to reality. Back in Israel. The couple makes its way out, watched closely by the audience. The man with the broad shoulders obviously wants to join them. I can see the battle raging under his turtleneck shirt, but he seems to feel it would be beneath him to be a follower. Someone tries to stop the couple, urging them to stay. "Enough is enough," the guy hisses. "People come here to have a good time, it's the weekend, you wanna clear your head, and this guy gives us Yom Kippur." His wife, her thick short legs teetering on stilettos, smiles helplessly and tugs her skirt down with one hand. When the man's look meets the medium, he hesitates for a second, lets go of his wife, walks past a few tables to her, and leans over and says gently: "I suggest you leave too, ma'am. This guy is not right, he's taking us all for a ride. He's even making fun of you."

Her lips tremble. "That's not true," she whispers, "I know him, he's just doing make-believe."

That whole time, onstage, Dovaleh watches the developments with his thumbs stuck in his red suspenders, nodding as though gleefully memorizing the man's words. As soon as the couple leaves, he hurries to the small blackboard and draws two more red lines; one of them is long and thick, topped with a pinhead.

After he puts down the chalk, he slowly and precisely circles around himself, eyes down, arms airplaned. Once, twice, three times, in the middle of the stage, a purification ritual of some kind. Then he flicks his eyes open like floodlights on a sports field: "But he's stubborn, the driver! Won't give up! He's looking for me, I can feel it, looking for my eyes, my ears. But me—I'm in my own bunker. I don't turn my head to him, don't give him any way to edge in. And the whole time my teeth are knocking to the beat, along with the windowpane. *Fu-ne-ral, fu-ne-ral, I'm-on-my-way-to-a-fu-ne-ral* . . . 'Cause listen, guys, I told you, I'd never in my life been to a single funeral up till then, and that is rattling me a fair bit, because how the hell do I know what it's going to be like?"

He pauses to examine the crowd. His demanding look turns defiant. I think he may be deliberately provoking them, daring them to get up and leave, to walk out on him and his story.

"Or a dead man," he adds softly. "Never seen that either. Or a dead woman."

"But look, amigos," he continues, seeming surprised that no one else has walked out, "let's not get all heavy with this funeral business, okay? We're not gonna let it bring us down. By the way, did you ever think there might be relatives who only meet at weddings and funerals, and so each of them is convinced all the others are manic-depressive?"

The crowd laughs judiciously.

"No, seriously, I was even thinking—you know how they have restaurant reviews and movie reviews in the paper? Well, I say, why not shiva reviews? They can get a critic to go to a different shiva every day and write up how it was, what was the atmosphere like, were there any juicy stories about the deceased, how the family behaved, if there was any fighting over the inheritance, and they'd rank the refreshments, and the class of mourners—"

Rolling laughter throughout the club.

"And if we're already in that vein, did you hear the one about the woman who goes to a funeral home and wants to see her husband before they bury him? So the undertaker shows her the husband and she sees they've put him in a black suit. By the way, this is not one of our jokes," he clarifies, holding a finger up, "it's translated from Christianese. So the woman starts weeping: 'My James would have wanted to be buried in a blue suit!' The guy says, 'Look, missus, we always bury them in black suits, but come back tomorrow and I'll see what I can do.' She comes back the next day and he shows her James in a gorgeous blue suit. The woman thanks him a thousand times and asks how he got hold of this great suit. Undertaker says, 'You won't believe this, but yesterday, not ten minutes after you left, another deceased came in, more or less your husband's build, in a blue suit, and his wife says his dream was to be buried in a black suit.' Well, James's widow thanks the undertaker again, she's really emotional, tears in her eyes. Gives him a huge tip. Undertaker says, 'All I had to do was switch the heads.'"

The crowd laughs. The crowd is back. The crowd gloats at the hasty departure of the shaved-head man from such a fabulous evening. "Everyone knows," says a woman at a nearby table, "that he's slow to warm up."

"So this whole drive is starting to get to me. My head's on fire from all the thoughts, everything's grinding, pounding, a whole mishmash inside my head, I'm so full of thoughts I can't find the way into my own mind. You know that thing where all your thoughts go flying around in one big fustercluck without any order, like before you go to bed? Just before you fall asleep? Did I shut the stove off or didn't I? I'm gonna have to get that cavity filled in my top molar. That chick rearranging her bra on the bus, she made my day. That son of a bitch Yoav said pay-ment terms are net ninety. Who even knows if I'll still be here in ninety days? Can a deaf cat catch a mute bird? Maybe it's a good thing none of my kids look like me. What are they thinking, chopping down trees without an anesthetic? Is a Chevra Kadi-sha driver allowed to put a bumper sticker on his hearse saying ON MY WAY WITH ANOTHER SATISFIED CUSTOMER? And what the hell was he thinking pulling Benayoun off the field ten minutes before the match ended? Can the notice say 'Dovaleh and Life Call It Quits'? I really shouldn't have had that mousse . . ."

Laughter—awkward, confused, but laughter. The rattling air conditioner pulls a fragrance of freshly cut grass into the room. There's no telling what planet it has come from. The smell is intoxicating. Memories of my little childhood house in Gedera wash over me.

"The driver says nothing. One minute, two minutes, how long can he go on? So he starts up again like we're deep into con-versation already. You know those characters who have no one to talk to? They're lonely, outcast? Those guys, they'll vacuum it out of you if they have to. I mean, you're their last chance, after you it's just those crosswalks that beep for the blind. Say you're sitting at the doctor's office at seven a.m. waiting for the nurse who draws blood?" The audience confirms its familiarity with the experience. "Now you're not even awake yet, haven't had your morning coffee, and you need at least three cups to even pry open your left eyelid, and all you really want is to be left alone to die in peace. But then the old guy next to you, with his fly open and his junk all out and the dark brown urine sample in his hand—by the way, have you ever noticed the way people walk around the clinic with their samples?"

People trade experiences, they're completely thawed out now, longing to heal. The medium giggles, steals embarrassed looks around, and he glances at her and a light passes over his lips.

"No, seriously, be serious for a minute. There's the ones who walk with their jar like this, right? The guy walks down the hallway on the way to the sample window. You're sitting on the row of chairs along the wall and he doesn't look in your direction. He's considering the lilies. He keeps the hand holding the sample on the other side of his body, as low as possible, am I right?"

The crowd confirms with squeals of delight.

"Like he actually believes that this way you can't even see that at the end of his hand he just happens to have a plastic jar, and the jar just happens to contain a piece of poop. Now zoom in on his face, yeah? It's like he's not even a party to this transaction, you know? He's just the messenger. He's actually a courier for the Mossad, and his hush-hush job is to transport biological cargo for R&D. I swear, those are the ones I like torturing best, especially if it's someone from the biz, an actor or a director or a playwright, one of those shits I used to work with when I was still alive. So anyway I jump right up at him with both arms out for a hug: 'Well hello, Mr. Bean!' Of course he pretends he doesn't remember me, has no clue where I've even turned up from. But what do I care? I've long ago forgotten if it's my dignity I lost or my shame. So I turn up the volume: 'Hola, amigo! What brings Your Honor to our humble clinic? Oh, incidentally, I read in the paper that you're cooking up a new masterpiece for us. Great news! We're all so curious to find out what you've produced! Your work is such a pleasure because it always comes from the inside, right? From the gut!'"

People are sputtering now, wiping away tears, hands slapping thighs. Even the stage manager hiccups a few laughs. The tiny woman is the only one not laughing.

"Oh, come on, what is it now?" he asks her after the hoots die down.

"You're embarrassing him," she says, and he gives me a helpless look: What are we going to do about her? That's when it hits me: Eurycleia.

I've been trying to remember the name since the minute it turned out the little lady knew him from childhood, and that she was tilting the direction of the whole evening. Eurycleia. Odysseus's elderly nanny, who bathed his feet when he returned from his voyage disguised as a beggar. She was the one who saw his childhood scar and recognized him.

I write the name on a napkin in block letters. For some reason this little remembrance makes me happy. And immediately I ask myself what I can give him here. What can I be for him?

I order another shot of tequila. I haven't drunk like this for years, and I have a yen for stuffed vegetables. And olives. A few minutes ago I didn't think I could put anything else in my mouth, but it turns out I was wrong. The blood is suddenly pumping through my veins. It's good that I came, really, it's good, and even better that I stayed.

"And then, after a few miles . . . Are you with me?" He pokes his face out at us as if through the window of a driving car, and we, meaning the audience, laugh and confirm that yes, we're with him, even though a few people around here seem surprised to find it so.

"Suddenly the driver goes, 'Hey, kid, I don't know if you're in the mood for this now, but next month I'm representing our command in an IDF-wide contest.'

"I don't answer. What am I supposed to say? At most I kind of grunt a *hmmm* under the mustache I don't have. But a few seconds later I feel a bit sorry for him, I don't know, maybe 'cause he looks so needy, so I ask him if it's a driving contest.

" 'Driving?' he exclaims. Then he rolls around laughing, baring his buckteeth: 'Me, in a driving contest?! I've got seventy-three citations, dude! I spent six months inside, added on to my service. Get out of here . . . Driving! I'm talking about a joke contest.'

"And I go, 'What?!' Because I swear I thought I hadn't heard right. And he says: 'Jokes, where you tell jokes, they do a competition every year, with the whole army.'

"Honestly, I was kind of in shock. Where the hell did he come up with that all of a sudden? And all this time I'm sitting there expecting that any minute he's going to tell me. You know? That he'll realize what's going on and he'll tell me. And now he comes out with this business about jokes?

"So we're driving. Not talking. Maybe he's hurt that I'm not taking an interest, but really, I'm not in the mood. And now I also start to notice what a terrible driver he is, how he's veering all over the place, onto the shoulders, into every pothole. Then I get the thought that my mother, if she was here, would probably tell me to wish him luck in the contest. I practically can't breathe from that thought. I hear her voice, the music of her speech. I can actually feel her breath on my ear, and I say, 'Best of luck with that.'

" 'There was maybe twenty guys in the tryouts,' he says, 'from all the bases, the whole Southern Command, and three of us made it to the finals, and then it was just me left to represent the command.'

" 'But how did they test you?' I ask. Just for her, I ask, because what the fuck do I care how they tested them, but I know she'd feel sorry for him because of the teeth and the zits and the whole way he looks.

"'They just did,' he says. 'I don't know, you know, we came into this room with a desk and we told them jokes. By topic.'

"So now here's the deal: I can tell the driver's talking with me, but he's somewhere else. His forehead is wrinkled and he's got the chain from his dog tags between his teeth, and I'm getting ready for this maybe being a red herring, this whole contest story. Maybe now, when I've let my guard down, he's suddenly going to stick me with it. Like a knife it'll come.

"'There was this one judge there, a reporter for *Bamahaneh*,' he goes on, 'and one guy from the Gashash was there, too—it was Shaike, the big one who always laughs. And there were two other comedians for judges, too, I don't know who they were. They throw us a topic and we do a joke.'

"'Yeah, sure,' I go. I can tell by his voice that he's lying, and I'm waiting for him to finish up his crap and tell me already.

"'So like they say: Blondes! And you have thirty seconds to deliver.'

"'Blondes'?"

Dovaleh stares into space again, his reliable trick. His eyelids are halfway down, and his face is frozen in bewilderment at the corrupt nature of man. The more he does it, the louder the audience laughs, but the laughter is hesitant again, unraveling. I sense a slight despair rippling through the audience as people realize that the man onstage is going to insist on his story after all.

"Meanwhile, the truck's dancing all over the road, and I know that means Jokerman is thinking, forgetting himself. Good thing the road is practically empty, there's barely another car every fifteen minutes. With my right hand I look for the door handle, feel its spring, squeeze it back and forth. I start getting a thought.

"'Look, kid,' the driver goes, 'you're not in the mood for jokes now, but if you do feel like it . . . Maybe it could, I don't know, make you feel better?'

"Better how? I think, and my head almost explodes.

"'Look, just give me a topic,' he says. He puts both hands straight on the wheel, and I can tell he's not kidding. His whole face changes in an instant, and his ears are burning red. 'Throw out anything you want, doesn't have to be what we said, could be anything: mothers-in-law, politics, Moroccans, lawyers, fags, animals.'

"Now you have to understand, my friends—look, just focus on me for a minute—I'm stuck there for a few hours with an insane driver who's taking me to a funeral and is about to tell me jokes. I'm not sure if you've ever been in that situation . . ." A woman's voice off to my left whispers, "We've been in that situation for an hour and a half." Fortunately, Dovaleh doesn't hear her or the muffled guffaws in response.

"For the first time," he says very quietly, almost to himself, "for the first time I start to feel what it would be like to be an orphan, with no one watching out for me.

"So we're still driving. The vehicle is an oven. Sweat drips into my eyes. Be nice to him, my mom says in my ear again. Remember that every person only lives for a short time, and you have to make that time pleasant for him. I hear her and my brain goes crazy on me with pictures of her, pictures from my memories of her, and real photos, too, of her and of him, although more him than her, 'cause she almost never agrees to have her picture taken, she screams if he so much as points a camera at her. My brain is pouring out pictures I didn't even remember I remembered, pictures from when I was a baby, from my first six months, when I was alone with him. He used to take me everywhere. He sewed this little fabric sack thing, which was looped around his neck, there's a picture where you see him shaving a client with me hanging on his body in the sack, peeking out with one eye under his face. She wasn't with us then, I told you, she was here and there, she was at a convalescent home, that was what the official press release said." He tugs at the skin under his eye with one finger. "Here and there around the cuckoo's nest. Here and there at the vein tailor. But where were we, Netanya, where were we . . .

"Never mind, don't strain yourselves. Suddenly all at once I got really cold in that car. Even though we were in the middle of a *hamsin,* I got cold all over my body. I started really shaking, teeth chattering, and the driver gives me a look and I'm convinced a thousand percent that he's thinking: Should I tell him already? Shouldn't I? Should I tell him now, or play with him a little longer? And then I got even more stressed out, because what if he really does tell me? What if he tells me right there in the car when I'm alone with him? So I quickly tried to think about other things, anything to not hear him, but what came to me was something I'd never thought before, as if my brain was in on the plot against me, throwing out ideas and questions, like whether you can cut the same exact place again, and how did it happen to her anyway, and what did it happen with, and was she alone at home when it happened. And the thoughts kept flooding in. Like, did he come home early from the barbershop while I was away at camp and, if not, then who picked her up from the shuttle? Who could pick her up like I did? And how did I forget to ask him about that before I went to Be'er Ora, and how did they get along on their own while I was gone?

" 'Wildlife,' I say quickly to the driver. It comes out in a shout. And the driver says, 'Wildlife . . . Wildlife . . .' And even that word gives me a zap in the heart. Maybe it was a bad sign that I said it. Everything seems like a sign suddenly. Maybe even breathing is a sign.

" 'I'm on it,' the driver goes. His lips move, and I can see his brain starting to work. 'Okay. Got one. A little baby koala bear stands on a branch, spreads his arms out, jumps off, crashes on the ground. Picks himself up, climbs all the way back up, stands on the branch, spreads his arms, jumps off, and crashes. Picks himself up again, climbs up, does the whole thing over and over again. This goes on and on, and the whole time two birds are sitting over on the next branch watching him. Finally the one bird says to the other, Look, we're going to have to tell him he's adopted.' "

The audience laughs.

"Ah, you're laughing! Nice city, Netanya. I wouldn't say you're exactly rolling around, but laughter was certainly registered. It's too bad you weren't in the car instead of me, you would have made the driver happy. Because me, I just sit there without laughing or anything, just shaking like a dog in the corner of the pickup, and my first thought is why is he telling me a joke about parents and their misfit kid? But the driver, the second he finishes telling the joke, he starts laughing himself. But I mean, he really goes at it. Sounds like a donkey braying. Honestly, his laughter is way funnier than the joke. Maybe that's why they took him for the contest. I didn't laugh, and I could tell he was disappointed, but he wasn't about to give up. I couldn't get over how he didn't give up. How can someone be so dense? I thought.

" 'Okay, here's one that kills me,' he says. 'Every time I tell it

I have to stop myself from cracking up, 'cause they disqualify you for that. A horse walks into a bar and asks the barman for a Goldstar on tap. The barman pours him a pint, the horse downs it and asks for a whiskey. He drinks that, asks for a tequila. Drinks it. Gets a vodka shot and another beer . . .' This driver guy is prattling on with his thousand and one nights, and all I want is to get away from him, and my head is bouncing against the windowpane, and through the shaking I suddenly hear this voice from a distance, from the desert, and it's hard to hear exactly, but it's a bit like a song Mom used to sing me when I was little, three or four, I guess. I have no clue where it came from, I swear it wasn't from me, I hadn't thought of that song for years, she used to sing it when I couldn't fall asleep, or when I was sick, she'd pick me up, rock me back and forth, *Ay li luli lu, schlaf mein tiare schepseleh, mach tzu di kleine eigelech . . ."*

The room falls silent. The little tune evaporates like a curl of smoke.

"Now think about him." He shakes himself off and sternly presses on. "Good things, good things, think good things about him, where, what, here, got it, soccer players, run the players through my mind by team, first Israeli teams, then Europeans, then South Americans. I was a champ at that, thanks to him, so whatever comes to mind that's fine. From age five, from when I went into first grade, he started teaching me about soccer. He put his heart and soul into it. Okay, enough, now it's her turn. But she's not coming. He keeps jumping into my head again. Every time I think something about her—there he is. What now? Standing in the kitchen frying an omelet, maybe that's a good sign, a sign that he's at home and everything's okay with him, and then I catch myself: How is that a good sign, you dumbass? How could you possibly think that's a good sign?

Then he looks up from the omelet at me and grins like you grin for a camera, and he does his trick, he flips the omelet in the air and holds his other hand up high like a conductor, and suddenly it looks like he's sucking up to me a bit, but why would he do that? What could he need from me now? It's got nothing to do with me. But he keeps looking at me like it *is* about me, and I beg him to go away, to stop scaring me, what does he want from me? I wish he would at least not come alone, I don't want either of them coming on their own now. But noooo—not only doesn't he leave, he gets even more stuck there. Now he shows me himself in the jeans room, I told you about that place, and there's a table there with a square mesh and a long saw stuck to the table vertically—"

His voice gets raspy. He takes a sip from the flask.

"Why the saw? Who asked that? Oh, well hello there, table twelve! You're a teacher, aren't you? I can tell from your accent. Why the saw, you ask? But all the rest sounds plausible, does it, Miss Teacher? Three hundred pairs of velveteen pants from Marseille reeking of fish, which turned out to have the zippers on the back—*that* makes sense? And sending a kid of barely fourteen off like that without—"

His eyes are bloodshot. He makes a long exhalation with his cheeks puffed out and shakes his head from side to side. My own throat starts to burn. He drinks again. Big, fast gulps. I must remember what I was doing all that time in Be'er Ora while he was on his way to a funeral. But how can you remember details like that after so much time?

Nevertheless, I take myself out of this place. I have to put some order into things. I exhort myself. No discounts. With all my might I try to revive within me the boy I was then, but he keeps crumbling in my consciousness, refusing to be held, to exist, to be subjected to this investigation. I don't give up. I put all my strength into those minutes. They're not easy, these thoughts. Dovaleh still isn't talking. Maybe he senses that I'm not listening to him. But I force myself to at least ask the requisite questions: Did I think about him every few hours, after he left the base? I don't remember. Or once a day at least? I don't remember. When did I realize he wasn't coming back? I don't remember. How did it not occur to me to find out where he'd been taken? And did I feel relieved that he was gone, or glad, even? I don't remember. I don't!

All I know is those were the first days of my love for Liora, which dulled any other emotion or thought. I also know that after camp I did not go back to the math tutor. I informed my parents that I wasn't going back under any circumstances. I spoke firmly, with a boldness that alarmed them. They gave in, they folded, they blamed it on Liora's bad influence.

He stretches his arms out to the sides as far as he can, and his smile stretches with them. "But I'll tell you, Miss Teacher, you'll be surprised to learn that the saw actually did have a purpose. Because Daddy-o the tycoon dabbled in the fabric business. Yes, yes, with his own two hands he created his own brand in the field of recycled textiles, *schmattes*-dot-com. He bought and sold rags, a noble occupation for his free time, during lunch hour at the barbershop, another prestigious enterprise . . ."

There's been a rustle in the audience for a few moments. It's hard to tell exactly where it's coming from. Almost everyone I look at seems fascinated by the story and by the storyteller— fascinated despite themselves, perhaps, sometimes with an expression of aversion, even terror. Yet there is a hum, as if from a distant hive, that has been rising from the crowd for a few minutes.

"He used to drive around Jerusalem's neighborhoods on his Sachs moped buying rags, old clothes, shirts, pants . . ." He can hear it too now. His voice crescendos into the familiar ragman call: *"Alte zachen!"* He bribes the crowd unabashedly, feverishly, desperately: "Blaaan-kets, liiiiin-ens, tooooo-wels, coooom-for-ters, diiiiiiia-pers . . . After he washed them, he'd sort them out by fabric and size." The hum is now a murmur coming from all around the club, lapping in from every direction. "And what he did then—listen up, my friends, I'm getting to the point, don't go anywhere—he'd sit on the floor in the jeans room and deal out the rags like a deck of cards, superquick, one for you, one for you, chop-chop, a pile of this kind and a pile of that kind, it was a real undertaking, don't look down on it, and then he'd run the shirts and pants and coats from top to bottom on the saw and cut out the dregs, all the buttons and zippers and clips and buckles and snaps, they'd all fall onto the mesh—but don't worry, those he sold to a tailor in Mea Shearim, nothing was wasted in his universe—and then he'd pack up the rags in bundles of a hundred, I used to help him with that, I liked it, we'd count together, *Acht un neintzik, nein un neintzik, hundert!* And we'd tie the rags up together really tight with twine, and off he'd go to sell them to auto shops, printing houses, hospitals . . ."

The murmur dies down. The kitchen din stops, too. There is a deep silence, like the flash of nothingness before a huge rupture. Dovaleh is so immersed in the story that he apparently doesn't notice something simmering, and I'm afraid someone will actually hurt him, throw a glass or a bottle or even a chair at him. Anything could happen now. He stands downstage, too close to the audience, his arms hugging his narrow chest, a distant, transparent smile caressing his face: "Every single evening

I'd sit there next to Mom with her needle and nylons and do my homework and watch him use the saw. I remember the way he moved, and how his eyes got rounder and blacker, until he looked up and gazed at Mom and within a second he'd come back from wherever he'd been, back to being a human being, and there's Mom, hey Mom, look, Netanya . . ."

All at once, the club erupts. People stand up. Chairs are pushed back, an ashtray drops to the floor with a clang. Mumbles, grumbles, sighs of relief, and then voices roll in from outside that do not belong here, wild laughter, car doors slamming, groaning engines, and screeching tires. Dovaleh trots over to the board, the chalk in his hand flies like a conductor's baton. Five, eight. Ten. More and more, at least ten tables gone. It wasn't a coordinated move. Something ripened all at once in people, and they stream out like hurrying refugees, bottlenecking at the door. The man with the thick shoulders who pounded his table before passes by me and grunts at his wife: "Can you believe how he's using us to work out his hang-ups?" She answers: "Yeah, and what about the lokshen? And don't forget the used nylons! We got a full-on storytelling circle!"

Three minutes later most of the audience is gone, and the little club with its low ceiling seems to be panting in shock. Those of us still seated watch the last of the departees with a dulled weariness, some condemning, others jealous. But there are a few, not many, who sit up straighter in their chairs and turn back to Dovaleh expectantly, with renewed energy. He himself, his back to the exits, finishes marking the last red lines on the board, which now look like a madman's doodle. He puts the chalk down and turns to face the sparsely populated club, and to my surprise he looks relieved.

"Remember the driver?" he asks, as if the last few minutes

have not occurred at all. He replies on our behalf: "Yeah, we remember. So meanwhile the driver does not stop telling jokes. More and more of them, and I don't even hear him, I don't even laugh out of politeness anymore, I can't do it. But he's a rock, the performer from hell, nothing can break him, he can have a thousand people walk out of his car in the middle of a drive and he'll keep on telling jokes. I look at him from the side and see how his face has changed. It's tough now, dead serious, and he doesn't turn to me, doesn't try to catch my eye, just joke after joke after joke. And I'm thinking: What the fuck? What is his problem?

"This whole situation, what can I tell you, the drive, the driver, the drill sergeant who actually used the word 'orphan,' which is something that hasn't even entered my mind yet—hasn't penetrated at all! Keeps flying off me like a tripped circuit breaker. An orphan is someone who gets old all of a sudden, isn't it? Or some kind of cripple. An orphan is Eli Stieglitz from the ninth grade, whose dad worked at the Dead Sea factories and a crane fell on him and Eli talked with a stutter ever since. Does that mean I'll start stuttering, too? What sound does an orphan make? Is there a difference between an orphan without a father and an orphan without a mother?"

His hands are tightened into fists that he holds up in front of his mouth. People lean closer to hear better. There are so few of us. Scattered around the room.

"And believe me, Netanya, I don't want anything in my life to change. I've had things good up to now, the best in the world. Our apartment suddenly seems like heaven, even though it's small and dark and you can suffocate from the smell of rags and velveteen and all his cooking. I even liked that smell suddenly. Okay, so it sucked ass, and it was a nuthouse, and yes, I got beat up generously, okay, big deal, everyone got hit, so what, who didn't get hit back then? That's the way it was in those days! They didn't know any better! Did it do us any harm? Didn't we turn out just fine? Didn't we become human beings?"

His eyes are glazed. He looks as though the events were happening now, right at this minute.

"That's how families are. One minute they hug you, the next they beat the crap out of you with a belt, and it's all from love. Spare the rod, spoil the child. 'Believe me, Dovchu, sometimes a slap is worth a thousand words.' And there you have my father's compendium of jokes in its entirety." He wipes the sweat off his forehead with the back of his hand and attempts a smile. "Where were we, my little chickadees? What's up with you? You really do look like battered children. You're making me want to give you a back rub and sing you a lullaby. Did you hear the one about the snail who goes to the police? You didn't? You didn't hear this one either?! So the snail walks into a police station and says to the desk sergeant, 'Two turtles attacked me!' Desk sergeant opens up a file and says, 'Describe exactly what happened.' Snail says, 'I don't really remember, it all happened so fast.'"

The audience titters cautiously. I do, too. Not just from the joke. The laughter now is mostly an excuse to breathe.

"So listen, my hand is on the door handle this whole time. And the driver, without looking at me, he goes—"

The little woman suddenly squeaks cheerfully. He looks at her: "What happened, medium? Did I start being funny?"

"Yes, the joke with the snail is funny!"

"Really?" His eyes open wide with joy.

"Yes! Because of how he said it all happened so fast . . ."

He peers at her over his glasses. I know he's running through possible quips: Anyone ever tell you you're like a bank safe? You both have a ten-minute delay mechanism . . . But he just smiles at her and throws his hands up. "You're one of a kind, Pitz."

She straightens up, her short neck growing longer: "That's what you told me."

"That's what I told you?"

"Once I was crying, and you came down the street—"

"Why were you crying?"

"'Cause they hit me, and you said—"

"Why did they hit you?"

"Because I weren't growing, and you came behind the house by the gas balloons—"

"On my hands?"

"Of course. And you said I was one of a kind, and that if I cried 'cause of them, then you see it upside down, and it's like I'm laughing 'cause of me."

"You still remember that?"

"I have a long memory as compensation," she explains and nods three times.

"And now for something completely different!" he declares, but his shout is restrained this time, perhaps so as not to startle her. "Suddenly the driver slaps his forehead and goes: 'I can't believe what an idiot I am! You're probably not in the mood for all this joking around now, right? I just wanted to clear your head so you could forget for a while, but I shouldn't be like this, I'm sorry, okay? Forgive me? No hard feelings?' So I say, 'It's okay.' Then he says, 'You should sleep now. I'm done. Not another word out of me all the way to Be'er Sheva. Zip!'"

He gives us another reenactment of the drive: his body bobs up and down, bouncing on potholes, leaning right and left with the curves. The passenger's eyes slowly close, his head droops onto his chest over the bumpy road. Suddenly he startles: "I wasn't sleeping!" And immediately drips back slowly into sleep. He is subtle and accurate, a master of his art. The small crowd grins: it has been given a gift.

"And then, a second before I manage to fall asleep, the driver goes: 'Kid, can I ask you one more thing?' I don't answer. So much for sleeping. 'I just want to know,' he says, 'are you purposely stopping it?'

"'Stopping what?'

"'I don't know . . . *It*. Crying.'

"Right then and there I snap my mouth shut. I'm literally biting down. Not talking to him. I'd rather he tell another lousy joke than interfere. So we drive. Except that he, as you've already learned, is not one to give up easily. A minute later he asks me again if I'm holding it in or if I just don't feel like crying.

"To tell you the truth, I don't understand it myself anymore. The driver was right: I should be crying, that's what orphans do, isn't it? Or half orphans, I guess. But I have no tears, I have nothing, my body is like a shadow, no feelings at all. And also, how can I put this . . . It's like nothing can really start until I actually know. Isn't that so?"

He stops to wait for an answer from us, the remnants of his audience.

"Only my eyes," he goes on softly, "are on the verge of exploding the whole time, but not from tears. No tears. From pain, just deadly pain pressing against my eyes."

With the knuckles of both fists he crushes his eyes under his glasses. He rubs them for a long time, hard, like he's trying to poke his eyes out of their sockets.

"'In my family, may he rest in peace, there was a brother who died,' the driver tells me. 'Five years old, he drowned. And even though I never knew him, I always cry over him.'

"And he really did start crying the minute he talked about him. The tears ran down his face in a straight line. 'I don't get how you can be like that,' the driver says, and he can barely talk, he's sobbing like a kid. And I look at his tears, and he doesn't wipe them away, and the stripe wets his cheek and drips down onto his uniform shirt, and he doesn't wipe it, not with his hand or anything. The tears just flow unrestrained, as much as he wants. But not with me. It's like something in my brain is stopped up, stuck, I have a brain clog, but if the something could break free, then I could start. And this whole time, don't forget, I keep thinking that maybe he knows something, maybe he picked something up when he was in the commander's barracks, and why doesn't he tell me, and why don't I just ask him and be done with it, it's just two words, for God's sake, why don't I just shut my eyes hard and throw the question out and come what may?

"Hey, guys! Guys!" he suddenly raises his voice and waves his arms, and people in the audience—all of us, really—flinch as if we'd been shaken out of a dream. We laugh awkwardly. He takes the red handkerchief out of his pocket and mops his sweat, then pretends to wring out the handkerchief, whistling to himself. "You know what I was thinking? The human brain . . . It never stops working for a second. It works weekends, holidays, even Yom Kippur. Lousy labor contract that brain negotiated—what was it thinking? But what was I going to . . . Oh, yeah. Imagine there's a country somewhere in the world where the legal system works like this: the judge sits there, bangs his gavel, and declares: 'The defendant will now rise!' " He straightens up, stands stiffly, and slides me a look. "'The court finds you guilty of armed robbery, and hereby sentences you to thyroid cancer.' Or, let's say, a panel of three judges finds you guilty of rape and sentences you to Creutzfeldt-Jakob disease. Or they say this: 'The court is informed that the prosecution has entered a plea bargain with the defense, and so instead of that German dude, Alzheimer, the defendant will only undergo a stroke. And for tampering with evidence he'll get an irritable bowel.'"

The shrunken audience laughs halfheartedly and he gives us a sly sideways look. "You know how the minute you get a disease, especially if it's a really juicy one, the kind with excellent potential to develop, I mean, to degenerate, then every person you run into tries to prove to you how it's actually not that bad? On the contrary! They all know someone who heard about someone who's been living with MS or liver cancer for twenty years, and their lives are awesome! Never been better! And they make such a big deal convincing you how awesome and cool and super-duper it is that you start thinking you must have been an idiot not to get you some of that sclerosis ages ago! You could have had such a fabulous life together! You could have made such a great couple!"

With these words he breaks into a tap-dancing routine that ends with a *"Ta-daaam!"* and his arms spread wide, kneeling on one leg, sweat pouring down his face. No one in the audience is capable of clapping. People swallow drily and look at him with bewildered eyes.

"Okay, so we're off again. We're on the road, Jokerman and your disloyal servant—fuck, I'm so disloyal." He tries to get up from his bent knee, succeeding on the third try. "We're hot, we're dry, we have flies in our eyes, flies in our mouths. You know what? I take back what I said before: I don't think about that drive very much. I mean, not when I'm awake, only once in a while I get these flashbacks, the windowpane and the way my head rattled on it. Or how I kept seeing the driver covering his teeth with his lips. Or how there was a tiny hole in the upholstery of my seat, which I stuck my finger in almost the whole way, and it was foam rubber, and you'll laugh but I'd never seen that stuff before, 'cause in my house we had straw mattresses, and I liked the feeling of the foam rubber, and the whole time I was in the pickup I felt like it was some kind of magic substance from another place, this noble matter that was protecting me, and I imagined that the minute I took my finger out of the hole everything would fall in on me. That kind of crap is what stuck in my mind about that drive, to this day, and when it comes back it's usually at night, in my dreams, and then it's feature length, and it's kind of funny that it happens almost every night, can you imagine how boring that is— Yo, projector! Why do you keep showing the same movie?! And then the driver, without looking at me, suddenly goes: 'But you haven't told me yet who—'"

Dovaleh glares at us with those befuddled eyes. He stretches the corners of his lips exaggeratedly and tries to force us to smile with him. No one smiles. He opens his eyes even wider and blinks quickly. His face is completely clownish now. He bobs his head up and down a few times and mouths silently: Not funny? Really? That's it? I'm not funny anymore? I've finally lost it? He drops his head to his chest and conducts a silent exchange with himself, complete with hand gestures and hyperbolic facial expressions.

Then he falls silent. Still.

The little woman somehow knows what is coming before the rest of us do. She shrinks back and puts her hands over her face. The fist flies so fast that I hardly see it. I hear the click of teeth hitting one another, and his whole face seems to wrench away from his neck for an instant. His glasses fall to the floor. He doesn't alter his expression. Just breathes heavily in pain. With two fingers, he props up the corners of his mouth: Still not funny? Not at all?

The audience is frozen. The two bikers sit with their faces pulled taut and their ears pricked up, and it occurs to me that they knew this moment would come—that it's the reason they came.

Now he screams: "No? Not at all? No, no, no?" He slaps his face, ribs, stomach. The spectacle looks like a fight between at least two men. Within the whirlwind of limbs and expressions I recognize the countenance that has passed over his face more than once this evening: he is uniting with his abuser. Beating himself with another man's hands.

This human tempest continues for perhaps twenty seconds until he stops abruptly. His body, without moving, seems to pull back, avoiding itself in disgust. Then he shrugs his shoulders and turns to walk offstage through the door he entered from at the beginning of the evening. He marches like a paper cutout, knees lifted high, elbows slicing the air. On the third step he tramples his glasses. He doesn't stop; his shoulders lift briefly, then plunge back down. His back is to us, but I can picture the sneer at having just crushed his glasses, and the hateful whisper: *Putz.*

He's about to walk off and leave us with an unfinished story. One leg and half his body are already out the door. He stops. Half of him is still here. He tilts his face back to us just slightly, blinks expectantly, flashes a pleading grin. I straighten up quickly and laugh out loud. I am fully aware of how I sound, yet

I laugh again. A few other voices join me, feeble and frightened, but they're enough to bring him back.

He turns and skips back merrily, like a girl in a meadow, and on his way he leans down and picks up his crooked glasses with their shattered lenses and perches them on his nose, where they look like a percentage sign. Two threads of blood dribble down from his nostrils to his mouth and onto his shirt. "Now I really can't see you at all." He beams. "You're nothing but black blurs to me. You could all walk out and I wouldn't even know!"

As I guessed, and as he himself knew, and perhaps hoped, a group of four gets up and leaves, shock on their faces. Another three couples follow. They abandon the club hastily, without looking back. Dovaleh takes a step toward the blackboard, but then waves his hand in resignation.

"The road flies by!" he yells, tailing the deserters with his voice. "The driver's so worked up, his whole face is one big tic, blinking all over his body, hitting the wheel: 'Can't you at least tell me if it's Dad or Mom?'

"I sit there saying nothing. Nothing. We keep driving. Loads of potholes. I don't even know where we are or how much farther we have to go. The window pummels my ear, sun burns my face. It's hard to keep my eyes open. I shut the left one, then right, alternating. The world looks different every time I switch. Then there's a moment when I gather up all the strength I don't have and I say: 'Don't you know?'

" 'Me?' poor Jokerman shouts, almost losing the wheel. 'How the hell would I know?'

" 'You were in the room with them.'

" 'Not when they said . . . And after that they started fighting with me . . .'

"I start to breathe. The driver doesn't know. At least he wasn't keeping it from me. I glance at him sideways and he suddenly looks like an okay guy. Kind of screwed up but okay, and he was trying so hard to make me laugh, and maybe he's also stressed out by this drive, and by me, I mean, he has no idea what I might be capable of—I have no idea myself.

"And I also start thinking that now I really do have to wait until Be'er Sheva. Whoever comes to pick me up there has to know. They must have told them. I wonder if I should ask how far it is to Be'er Sheva. I'm getting hungry, too. I haven't had anything to eat since morning. I lean my head back and close my eyes. That lets me breathe a little, because suddenly I have more time: between now and when the Be'er Sheva people tell me, I can pretend nothing's happened and everything is just like it was when I left home, and I'm just taking a ride in a military truck to Be'er Sheva with a driver who's telling me jokes, because—why? Because that's what I feel like doing. Because there happens to be a joke contest today at HQ that I'm dying to see."

In the distance, from the industrial area outside the club, a siren wails. One of the waitresses sits down at an abandoned table and stares at Dovaleh. He gives her a weary smile: "Come on, look at you, dollface! What's up with you all again? Yoav won't pay me if you walk out of here looking like that. Why the long face? Did someone die? It's only stand-up comedy! Admittedly, this gig came out a little alternative, with some old-time army stories. And it's been donkey years since then—forty-three years, guys! There's a statute of limitations, and that kid has not been with us for ages, God bless his soul, I'm totally rehabilitated from him. Come on, smile a little, show me some consideration for once. For my need to make a living. For the alimony I gotta pay. Where are those law students?" He tents his hand over his crooked glasses, but the group left ages ago. "Okay," he grumbles, "never mind, maybe they had to get to a kangaroo court somewhere. By the way, do you know what 'alimony' means in Latin? The literal translation into Hebrew is 'method of extracting a male's testicle via his wallet.' Good stuff, heh? Poetic. Yeah, yeah, you can laugh . . . Me, I'm crying . . . There are women whose pregnancies don't take, but me, my marriages don't take. I want them, but they don't take. It's the same story every time. I make promises, I make vows, then I start up with my crap again, and then it's the usual mess, hearings, property distributions, visitation rights . . . Did you hear about the rabbit and the snake who fell into a dark pit together? You didn't hear about that either? Where are you living, guys?! So the snake feels the rabbit up and says, 'You have soft fur, long ears, and big front teeth—you're a rabbit!' The rabbit feels the snake up and says, 'You have a long forked tongue, you slither, and you're slippery—you're a lawyer!'"

He cuts off our feeble laughter with one finger held up. "Here's a question for you, a little Zen Dovism: If a man stands alone in the forest and there's not a single person or living creature around him, is it still his fault?"

Women laugh, men snicker.

"The driver starts banging his hand on the wheel, and he yells: 'What the hell! How could they not tell you? How didn't they tell you?' I don't answer. 'Fuckin' A,' he says and lights a cigarette, his hands trembling. He gives me a crooked sideways glance. 'Want one?' I pull one out of the pack like it's nothing. He lights it for me. My first real cigarette. It's a Time, the brand all the kids smoke. At camp the guys wouldn't give me any. 'You're still a kid,' they said. Passed it back and forth over my head. Even the girls passed it over me, and now the driver just lights it for me, and the lighter has a naked girl taking her clothes on and off. I inhale, I cough, it burns, it's good. I hope it burns everything. Hope it burns the whole world up.

"So now we're driving and smoking. Silently, like men. If Dad could see me, he'd slap me right there and then. So now it's her turn, quickly, doesn't matter what. Think of how her face looks when she gets off the Taas bus in the evening, like she's spent the whole day working for the angel of death, every day she's like that, never gets used to it, and only after she showers the smell of bullets off her body does she become human again. Then she sits in her armchair and I do my shows. 'The daily show,' we call it, and I plan it out every day on the way to school and during school and after school. It's a special show just for her, with characters, and costumes, hats, scarves, clothes I nick from the neighbors' laundry lines, stuff I find on the street— after all, I am my father's son.

"And it's dark all around us, but me and her, we don't need light. The little red light from the hot-water switch is enough. She does best in the dark, that's what she says, and her eyes really do get bigger in the dark, it's unreal. Like two blue fishes in the faint red glow. When you see her on the street with her scarf and boots, head down, you don't know how beautiful she is, but inside the house she's the most beautiful woman in the world. I used to do comedy sketch routines by the Gashash, and Uri Zohar and Shaike Ofir, and impersonations of the Theater Club Quartet. I'd use a broomstick for a microphone and I'd sing to her: 'That Means You're Young,' and 'My Beloved of the White Neck,' and 'He Didn't Know Her Name.' A whole show, every evening, for years, day after day, and he didn't know about it. He never caught us. Sometimes he'd come in a second after we finished, and he'd smell something, but he couldn't figure out what it was, and he'd stand there shaking his head at us like an old teacher, but that was it, never more, he couldn't even have imagined what she was like when she watched me."

He leans forward and bends like he's rounding his body over the story.

"And I start feeling like maybe it's wrong that I'm thinking about her for so long without a break, but on the other hand I don't want to stop in the middle, I'm afraid to weaken her. She's very weak as it is. His turn will come soon. There has to be justice. Equal time, down to the second. She used to sit with her feet on the little ottoman, with a white robe and a white towel twisted around her head. Like a princess, she looked. Like Grace Kelly." He turns to face us and his voice suddenly sounds different: the clear voice of a man simply talking to us. "Look, maybe it was only an hour a day, total, the time I had with her alone, until he came home. Maybe even less than an hour, maybe fifteen minutes, I don't know, when you're a kid time passes differently. But those were my best moments with her, so maybe I inflated them a little . . ." He chuckles. "I used to do all kinds of routines for her: 'The food here is terrible, and the portions are so small!' 'I shot a moose once.' And all the Israeli classics, too. She'd sit there with her cigarette like this, with her smile that's half on you, half behind your head, and I don't even know what she could understand from all my Hebrew and the accents and the slang, she probably missed a lot of it, but every single evening, for three or four years, maybe five, she would sit there and watch me, smiling, no one else but me saw her smile like that, I guarantee you, until suddenly she'd get sick of it all at once, in midword, didn't matter where I was, I could be at the tip of the point of the punch line and I'd see it coming, I was an expert, her eyes would start escaping inward, her lips would tremble, her mouth moved sideways, so I'd rush to the punch line, try to round the corner, I'd sprint, but I could see her face close off right in front of my eyes, and that was it. The end. Nothing. I'm still standing there with the scarves on my head, holding a broom, feeling like a total idiot, a jester, and she's flinging the towel off her head and putting out the cigarette. 'What will become of you!' she'd yell. 'Go do your homework, go out and play with your friends . . .'"

It takes him three rotations around the stage to get his breath back, and during the lull I find myself wallowing in pain from a different place. If only I had a child from her, I think for the thousandth time. But this time it stabs me somewhere new, in an organ I never knew I had. If only I had a child who would remind me of her in some small way—in the curve of her cheek, in a single movement of her mouth. That's all. I swear, I wouldn't need anything more.

"Anyhoo, where were we?" he shouts hoarsely. "Where was I? Let's go, nose to the grindstone, Dovaleh. We covered Be'er Ora, driver, cigarette, Mom, Dad . . . So we're driving fast, the speedometer's at seventy-five, eighty miles an hour, the chassis is starting to vibrate, but the driver won't stop banging his fist on the wheel and shaking his head. Only time I've seen one of those bobbleheads driving instead of sitting on the dashboard. Every few seconds he gives me a twisted look, like I'm . . . like I have some, I don't know, some disease . . .

"But me, nothing. Smoking. I take deep drags, burning my brains real good, all my thoughts. But on the other hand, if I smoke I can think about them without really thinking, because she smokes, too, and he does, she in the evening, he in the morning, and just from that thought the smoke from both of them blends together and my head fills with smoke, like there's a fire in there, and I flick the cigarette out the window and I can't breathe—I can't breathe."

He walks distractedly all over the stage, fanning his face. There are moments when I think he's drawing strength from the story. Yet a second later I feel the story sucking all the vitality out of him. I'm not sure if it's connected, but perhaps because of the way he moves with the story, something emerges in me, an idea: maybe I'll write down for him, briefly, in bullet points, a description of this evening. I'll just sit at home with my scribbled napkins and try to write down what happened here in an organized way.

For him to have. A souvenir.

"And suddenly he stops the truck, Jokerman. But not like delicately sliding over—no, he screeches the brakes like a bank robber!" He demonstrates, lurching forward and slamming back, his mouth gaping: "Steve McQueen in *Bullitt*! Bonnie and Clyde! Onto the shoulder—no, wait, there's no shoulder! This is forty-three years ago, they'd barely invented roads, people still clapped when they saw a car crash, asked for encores! *Boom!* The truck jolts, the two of us bounce up and bang our heads on this kind of canvas roof with a metal frame, we shout, our teeth are castanets, mouths full of sand, and when the truck finally comes to a stop he slams his head on the horn—just rams into it with his forehead. I'm telling you, maybe thirty seconds he sat there like that, ripped a hole through the desert. Then he lifts his head up and pounds one fist on the wheel so hard I'm afraid he's going to shatter it, and he goes: 'What do you say we go back?'

" 'What do you mean, back? I gotta get to Jerusalem.'

" 'But it's not right that you don't . . . ,' he starts stammering. 'It's against the . . . I don't know, it's against God even, or like the Torah. It's wrong, I can't keep driving like this, it's making me feel bad, for real, it's making me sick . . .'

" 'Keep driving,' I tell him like my voice has already changed. 'They'll tell us in Be'er Sheva.'

" 'Fuck they will!' He spits out the window. 'Those shits, I got their number already. Bunch of pussies. Each one's gonna try and make the other guy tell you.'

"Then he gets out to take a piss. I sit in the truck. Alone, suddenly. It's the first moment I've been like that, with just myself, since the sergeant woman left me in front of the commander's barracks. And immediately I can see—it's not good for me, being alone. It crowds in on me. I open the door and jump down to pee on the other side of the truck. I stand there peeing and a second later he jumps into my head, my father, shoves himself in there, he does that more than she does—what does that mean and why is she growing weaker on me? I force her back in, but he comes with her, trailing her, won't leave me alone with her for a second. What the fuck. I think about her hard, I want to see her the good way, but what do I get instead? I see the way she goes white when the radio says Israeli soldiers killed a terrorist, or there was an exchange of fire and a whole unit was wiped out by our forces. When she hears that, she gets up quickly and goes into the bathroom. Even if she already washed before that, she goes in and starts all over again, stays there maybe an hour, scrubbing the skin off her hands, using up all the hot water, and Dad gets annoyed and paces the hallway, fuming—*Psssh! Psssh!* At the hot water and at how she doesn't support our army. But when she comes out he doesn't say a word. Not a word. There, I've thought about him again, he won't let me be alone with her for a second."

He wanders around the stage. I think his feet are faltering

slightly. The copper urn behind him imbibes and spits out his reflection over and over again feverishly.

"My mind is racing: what's going to happen, how will things work out, what'll happen to me, who'll take care of me. Just as an example, you know, when I was about five he started teaching me soccer, I told you, not how to play, you must be kidding, he wasn't interested in playing, but he taught me the facts, the rules, and results from the World Cup and the Israel Cup and tournaments and names of players in the national league, and then the teams from England and Brazil and Argentina, and Hungary, obviously, and the whole world, except Germany, of course, and except Spain because of the Expulsion, which he still hadn't entirely forgiven them for. Sometimes when I'm doing my homework and he's sawing his *schmattes,* he suddenly shoots at me: 'France! Mondial '58!' And I shoot back: 'Fontaine! Jonquet! Roger Marche!' Then he says: 'Sweden!' And I say: 'What year?' And he goes: 'Also 1958!' So I say: 'Liedholm! Simonsson!' It was good times with him. Just so you know, the guy never went to a soccer match in his life. Thought it was a waste of time: Why do they have to play for ninety minutes? Why not twenty? Why not stop at the first goal? But he got it in his mind that I was small and weak, and that if I knew a lot about soccer the boys would respect me and protect me and not beat me up too much. That's how his mind worked, always an ulterior motive, a trick up his sleeve, you never knew exactly where you stood with him—is he for you? Against you? And I think that's how he brought me up, too, to believe that ultimately everyone watches out for himself. That was his mantra in life, the essence of the legacy passed down by Daddy-o to his tender son.

"What were we talking about, Netanya? What else do I remember? Oh, sure, I remember loads, I'm just now realizing how much I remember. Too much. Like after I finished pissing I did just like he taught me, 'Shake once, shake twice,' and then it occurred to me that he taught me quite a lot of things just incidentally, without making a big deal out of it, like how to fix a blind and drill holes in the wall and clean out a kerosene heater and unclog a drain and make fuse wires. And I also thought about how sometimes I had the feeling he was dying to talk to me about things, not just about soccer, which he didn't really care about—I mean about other things between a father and son, like his childhood memories, that kind of stuff, or thoughts, or just to come over and give me a hug. But he didn't know how to, or maybe he was embarrassed, or maybe he just felt like he'd left me with Mom too much and now it was hard to change, and then I realize I'm thinking about him again instead of her, and my head starts spinning with all that crap and I can barely climb back into the truck.

"Good evening, Netanya!" he roars as if he's only just burst onto the stage, but his voice is tired and raspy. "Are you still with me? Do you by any chance remember—who's old enough in here to remember? When we were kids we had this toy, the View-Master? It was this little thing with slides, where you'd press down and the pictures would switch. That was from back in the golden age of cellulite," he quips, "that's how we saw Pinocchio, and Sleeping Beauty, and Puss in Boots . . ."

Only two members of the audience smile—the tall silver-haired woman and me. Our eyes meet for a moment. She has a delicate face and thin-framed glasses.

"So that's how you can see me now. Me and the driver in the truck, *click*. Around us the desert, *click*. Every so often a military vehicle comes toward us and then there's that zoom when you pass each other, *click*."

A group of five young men and women sitting close to the stage look at one another, get up, and leave. They don't say a word. I don't know why they stayed this long, or what made them leave at this particular moment. Dovaleh walks over to the blackboard and stands there. I sense that this abandonment is more hurtful to him than the others. Shoulders hunched, he slams the chalk down on the board: line, line, line, line, line.

But then right at the exit door, one of the women stops, the one without a boyfriend, and despite her friends' cajoling, she says goodbye to them and sits down at an empty table. The manager signals for the waitress to go over to her. She asks for a glass of water. Dovaleh lopes back to the board like a camel—a flicker of Groucho Marx—and makes a big show of erasing one of the lines. As he does so he turns his head back and gives her a big openmouthed grin.

"And all of a sudden, without thinking, I say to the driver: 'Tell me a joke.' And his whole body folds over like I've punched him. 'Are you a sicko? A joke, now?' 'What do you care? Just one joke,' I reply. 'No, no, I can't do it now.' 'Then how come you could before?' 'Before I didn't know. Now I know.' He doesn't even turn his head. Afraid to look at me. Like he's scared he'll get infected. 'Forget it,' he says, 'my head's exploding enough already from what you told me.' 'Do me a favor,' I say, 'just one joke about a blonde. What's the worst that could happen? It's just you and me in the car, no one will know.' But he goes, 'No, swear to God, I can't do it.'

"Well, if he can't do it, he can't do it. So I leave him alone. Put my head on the window and try wiping my brain out all the way, *drrrr*, no thinking, no being, no nothing, no she, no he, no orphan. Yeah, right. The second I shut my eyes my dad jumps on me, he's turned into a commando now, doesn't even wait a second. On Fridays, when Mom works the morning shift, he wakes me up early and we go out to the garden. I told you this, right? I didn't? It was just ours, that garden, behind the building, tiny—maybe three by three. All our vegetables came from there. And we sit there wrapped in a blanket, him with his coffee and cigarette and his black stubble, me half asleep, kind of almost leaning on him as if I didn't realize it, and he dips biscuits in the coffee and feeds them to me, and it's completely silent around us. The whole building is asleep upstairs, no one's moving in the apartments, and the two of us barely say anything."

He holds one finger up so we can hear the silence.

"At that time of the morning, he doesn't have the *zzzzap* in his body, so we look at the dawn birds and the butterflies and beetles. We throw biscuit crumbs for the birds. He can make birdcalls where you can't believe it's a human being whistling.

"Suddenly I hear the driver talking. 'There's a shipwreck, and only one person manages to jump off and swim. He swims, he splutters, he swims. Finally, when he's totally worn out, he drags himself onto an island, and sees that he's not alone: a dog and a goat managed to swim over, too.'

"I half open my eyes. The driver talks without moving his lips, you can barely understand him.

"'A week goes by, two weeks, the island's empty, no people, no animals, just the guy and the goat and the dog.'

"It sounds like the driver's telling a joke, but it's not a joke voice. He talks like his whole mouth is a pulled muscle.

"'After a month the guy's horny as all heck. Looks to the right, looks to the left, not a female in sight, only the goat. After another week, the guy can't take it anymore, he's gonna burst.'

"And I start thinking: Pay attention, this driver is telling you a dirty joke. What the hell is going on? I open another half eye.

Jokerman's got his whole body hunched over the wheel, his face is stuck to the windshield, dead serious. I shut my eyes. There's something here that I need to understand, but who has the strength to understand, so I just draw a picture in my mind of the island with the guy and the goat and the dog, planting a nice palm tree, cracking open a coconut, hanging up a hammock. Deck chair. Beach ball.

"'Another week goes by and the guy can't take it anymore. So he goes over to the goat and pulls his junk out, but suddenly the dog gets up and goes, *Grrrrr!* Like he's saying: Watch it, brother, don't touch the goat! Well, the guy gets scared, packs it up, and thinks: At night the dog'll go to sleep and I'll make my move. It's night, the dog's snoring, the dude quietly crawls over to the goat. He's just getting on her when the dog pounces like a panther, barks like crazy, his eyes are like blood, teeth like knives. So the poor guy—what choice does he have? Crawls back to sleep with blue balls up to his eyelids.'"

Dovaleh talks and I look around at the people. At the women. I glance at the tall woman. Her short-cropped hair is like a halo around her lovely, sculpted head. Three years. Since Tamara got sick. Total apathy. I wonder if women are somehow able to sense what's happening to me, and if that's the reason it's been so long since I've picked up any sort of sign from a single one of them.

"You gotta understand that I've never heard anyone tell a joke that way in my life. He squeezes out every word like if God forbid he skips a single syllable they'll disqualify his entry and revoke his joke-telling license for the rest of his life."

Dovaleh imitates the driver down to the finest detail, his whole body hovering in front of us as he folds over an invisible wheel. "'And it goes on like that another day, another day, a week, a month. Every time the guy gets anywhere near the goat, the dog jumps up: *Grrrr!*' "

Smiles here and there. The little woman giggles and puts her hand over her mouth. *"Grrrrr!"* Dovaleh growls again, only to her, a variation on the *drrrrr* from before. She loves it. Her laughter rolls out like he's tickled her. He looks at her tenderly.

" 'One day, the guy's sitting there looking out at the sea in despair, when suddenly he sees smoke in the distance—another ship is sinking! And out of the ship jumps a blonde, and she is fully equipped: everything's in the right place, plenty for him to work with. The guy doesn't hesitate for a second—jumps in, swims all the way out, gets to the blonde. She's almost drowning, he grabs her, drags her to the island, lays her down on the sand, she opens her eyes, and she's gorgeous, she's like a model, and she says: "My hero! I'm all yours. You can do anything you want to me!" So the guy looks around suspiciously and says quietly, in her ear, "Listen, lady, would you mind holding the dog for a minute?" '

"But me—no, listen, Netanya!" He doesn't even let us laugh properly, the way we all very much need to. "I suddenly burst out laughing so hard, I was literally screaming in that pickup because of all the . . . I don't know . . . because my brain was so fried from the whole situation, or from not thinking for two whole minutes about what was waiting for me soon. Maybe also because someone older than me had told me a grown-up joke, he'd given me credit for being in the know. But then my brain kicks in with its crap, and I'm thinking what does it mean that the driver thinks I'm an adult already? Maybe I don't want to be a grown-up so quickly?

"But the point is that I laughed until tears came from my eyes, I swear, the tears finally came, and I hoped that counted.

And with everything so fucked up I start feeling like it's actually good for me to think about the blonde who almost drowned, and about the dog and the goat, and I see them in front of my eyes on their hammocks with the coconuts, and it's better than thinking about anyone I know.

"But the driver, I could see it was stressing him out to hear me laugh like a nutcase, maybe he was scared I was losing it, but on the other hand he was also tickled that I liked his joke, how could he not be, and he sat up straight and licked his teeth quickly, he had this kind of mannerism, actually he had all kinds of mannerisms, I still think of him sometimes to this day, the way he kept shifting his sunglasses on his forehead, or pinching his nose with two fingers to make it smaller. 'Ben-Gurion, Nasser, and Khrushchev are flying in a plane,' he says quickly before I can go cold on him. 'Suddenly the pilot announces they're out of fuel and there's only one parachute . . .'

"What can I tell you, the guy was a walking jokebook. He knew a helluva lot more about jokes than about driving, that's for sure. And I figured, What do I care? Let him go on like that all the way to Be'er Sheva, where they'll tell me, they can't not, that's where the orphan thing will really start, but until we get there I have a reprieve, like I got pardoned, that's how I felt, like I got a stay of execution for a few minutes."

Dovaleh holds his head up and looks at me for a long time, nodding. And I remember how alarmed he was, horrified even, when I asked him on the phone if he was asking me to judge him.

"And the same goes for him, the driver. I think he was happy to keep going with the jokes, partly because of the stress about me, but maybe also because he just wanted to make me feel good. Either way, from that moment on he didn't even take a breather, lit each joke with the last one, just filled me good and well with jokes, and honestly, I don't even remember most of them, but a few stuck, and the guys sitting at the bar—Hey, guys! You're from Rosh Ha'ayin, right? Oh, sorry, of course, Petach Tikva. Respect!—they've been with me for fifteen years at least. Cheers, muchachos! And they know that those are the two or three jokes I work into every show, whether I need to or not, so now you know where they come from, like that one about the guy who had a parrot who wouldn't stop cussing? Listen to this, you'll like this one. From the second he opened his eyes in the morning until he went to sleep, he let out the juiciest—

"What's the matter?" he bites his lip. "Did I screw up? No, wait, don't tell me I already told you that one tonight?"

People sit there motionless, eyes glazing over.

"You already told us about that parrot," says the medium without looking at him.

"No, it's a different parrot . . . ," he mumbles. "Just kidding! Psych! Sometimes I like to test the crowd to see if they're awake. You passed! You're an outstanding audience!" He grimaces and his face falls in fear. "Where was I?"

"With that Jokerman," says the little woman.

"It's the meds," he says to her and sucks thirstily from his thermos.

"Side effects," she says, still without looking at him. "I have them, too."

"Listen, Pitz," he says. "Guys, look, I'm almost done, just stay with me awhile longer, okay? So the driver's churning out jokes and cracking himself up, and my head is one big fustercluck, the priest, the rabbi, and the prostitute, and the sheep who sings from the *mohel*'s stomach, who accidentally switched backpacks with the lumberjack, and the parrot—the second parrot,

I mean—and they all get mixed up with the whole day's craziness, and I guess at some point I fell asleep.

"And when I wake up, what do I see? That we're stopped in some place that is definitely not the Be'er Sheva Central Bus Station. Just a yard with chickens clucking around, and dogs scratching themselves, and doves in a birdcage, and next to the car stands this thin woman with a pile of black curls, and she's holding a thin baby in a diaper. She stands next to my window looking at me like she's seeing a two-headed beast. And the first thing I think is: What's on that chick's face? What's she got painted on? And then I realize it's tears. She has actual tears coming down in straight lines without stopping, and the driver stands next to her with a sandwich in his mouth, and he looks at me and says, 'Good Morning, America! This is my big sister. She's coming with us. Can you believe she's never been to the Wailing Wall? But first we'll get you where you need to go, don't worry.'

"What the hell?! Where am I, what am I, *what* Wailing Wall— that's in Jerusalem! Where's Be'er Sheva? How did we get here?

"The driver laughs: 'You were out cold half the way here. I put you to sleep like a baby with my jokes.' And the woman says, 'I don't believe it—you've been torturing him with your one-liners, you dipshit? Aren't you ashamed to tell him jokes in his state?'

"Despite the tears, she has a tough, irritable voice. And the driver says to her: 'Even when he was asleep I told them. I didn't leave him jokeless for a second. Man-to-man defense, I gave him. Now get in.' She sits down in the back of the truck with the baby and a big bag. 'We passed Be'er Sheva ages ago,' he tells me, 'I'm not letting you make this trip alone, kid. You got into my heart, I'm taking you door-to-door all the way home.' 'But do me a favor,' his sister says, 'no more jokes. And don't look, I have to nurse him. Turn that mirror away—pervert!' She gives him a little slap from behind, and I sit there like an idiot and think: Why the hell won't they let my orphanhood start? They keep putting it off. Is it a sign that I'm supposed to do something? But what?"

He slowly walks to the red armchair and perches on the edge. You can see that his eyes, behind his cracked lenses, are looking inward. I scan the club on his behalf. Maybe fifteen of us are left. A few of the women stare at him with a look both distant and focused, as if they're seeing through him to another time. It's hard to mistake that look: they know him intimately, or once did. I wonder what made them come here tonight. Did he phone each one of them and invite her? Or do they always turn up at his shows when he comes through town?

I realize there's something missing in the picture: the two young bikers' table is empty. I didn't see them leave. I guess after his barrage of punches they assumed that was the most they'd get.

"So I sit there with my face to the windshield. Dying of fear that my eye will roam to the backseat. I mean, at least she was sitting in the back, but this new thing where every other woman starts breast-feeding in public . . . ? I mean, think about it, it's not funny at all, you're standing with a woman, she looks totally normal, normative, as they say, and she's got her baby on her hip, and never mind that to you he looks eight years old, he's already got stubble—"

His voice sounds hollow, almost toneless.

"—so you and she are just chatting about current affairs, discussing the quantum theory of relativity, when all of a sudden, without batting an eyelid, she pulls a breast out of her sleeve!

A real breast! Manufacturer certified! And she sticks it in the baby's mouth and keeps on talking to you about the electromagnetic particle accelerator in Switzerland . . ."

He's saying goodbye. I can feel it. He knows this is the last time he's going to tell these jokes. The girl who was about to leave but came back leans her head on one hand and gazes at him vaguely. What's her story? Did she go home with him after a gig one night? Or maybe she's one of his five children, and this is the first time she's hearing his story? And the two bikers in black—were they somehow connected to him as well?

I remember what he told us before, about how he used to play chess with people walking on the street. They each had a role, even though they didn't know it. Who knows what complicated chess game he's conducting simultaneously here tonight?

"And the girl, his sister, keeps nursing the baby, and at the same time I hear her digging around in her bag with one hand, and she says to me: 'I bet you haven't had anything to eat all day. Give me your hand, kid.' I reach my hand back and she puts a wrapped sandwich in it, and then a peeled hard-boiled egg and a little screw of newspaper with some salt for the egg. As tough as she looks, her hand is really soft inside. 'Eat,' she says. 'How could they send you off like this with nothing to put in you?'

"I scarf down the sandwich, and it has delicious, thick salami and spicy tomato spread that burns my mouth, and it's good, it kicks me awake, puts me back in the game. I sprinkle salt on the egg and finish it off in two bites. Without talking, she passes me a savory cookie and takes a family-sized bottle out of her bag—I swear, this chick was Mary Poppins—and gives me a cup of orangeade. How she does all that with one hand, I cannot understand, and how she manages to feed the baby and me at the same time, I understand even less. 'The cookies are a little dry,' she says, 'wash them down with the orangeade.' I do everything she tells me."

Dovaleh's voice—what's happening to it? It's hard to make out the words, but in the last few minutes the voice itself is thin and floating, almost like a child's.

"And the driver, her brother, reaches his hand back, too, and she puts a cookie in it. And he reaches back again, and again. I feel like he's doing it to make me laugh because she won't let him tell me any jokes. We drive without talking. 'No more cookies,' she says, 'you're being greedy, leave some for him.' But he keeps holding his hand out, and he winks at me with his mouth full, and she slaps him on the back of the neck and he shouts 'Ouch!' and laughs. When my father gives me that slap, after he cuts my hair, I both anticipate it and slightly fear it. A stinging little slap, after the cotton ball with the aftershave. He does it with the tips of his fingers, and then he whispers in my ear so the clients won't hear, 'Handsome cut, *mein leibn,* my life.' And now it's her turn. Good things about her. But what's best to think about her now? What would help most? I'm suddenly afraid to think about her. I don't know, she's gone colorless on me. What am I doing wrong? I force her back in. She doesn't want to come. I tug hard, pull her in with both hands, I have to have her in my mind, too. It can't be just him. Don't give up! I yell at her. Don't surrender! I'm almost sobbing, doubling my whole body over against the car door so the driver and his sister won't see, and here she comes, thank God, sitting in the kitchen with a pile of nylons to darn. And there I am sitting next to her doing my homework, and everything's normal, and she hooks eye after eye with the needle, and every few eyes she stops, forgets herself, stares into space, doesn't see the darning or me. What is she thinking about when she does that? I never asked her. A thousand times I was alone with her and I never asked. What do I know? Almost nothing. Her parents were wealthy, I know that from Dad. She was an excellent student, she played the piano, there was talk of recitals, but that was it, she finished the Shoah when she was twenty and she'd spent six months of the war in a single train car, I told you that. They hid her there for half a year, three Polish train engineers in a little compartment on a train that ran back and forth on the same tracks. They took turns guarding her; she told me that once, and she gave this crooked laugh I'd never heard before. I must have been twelve or so, and it was just me and her alone at home, and I did a show for her when she suddenly stopped me and told me the whole story in one go, and her mouth twisted sideways and she couldn't straighten it out for a few seconds, this whole part of her face spilled to one side. After six months they decided they'd had enough of her. I don't know why, don't know what happened one fine day when they got to the last stop and those louses threw her out straight onto the gatehouse ramp.

"Should I go on?" he asks in a strained voice. A few heads nod.

"I can't remember the exact order, a lot of things get mixed up in my mind, but for example there's always the way I hear his sister in the backseat saying to herself quietly, 'God help us,' and I generally get the feeling that the sister, her mind is working all the time. Grinding away. She has thoughts about me and I don't know what they are. Before, when she stood outside the truck looking in, I saw two deep, black grooves down her forehead. I sink deeper in my seat so I won't be in her eyes. I can hear the baby sucking the whole time, and every few sucks he sighs like an old man, and that stresses me out. They're taking care of him, protecting him, giving him what he needs, so why is he sighing? Then out of nowhere the sister says, 'Your dad, what's his job?'

" 'He has a barbershop. Him and a partner.' I don't know why I told her about that. I'm an idiot. Any second I might have told her how Dad likes to joke about the partner being in love with Mom, and how he plays around with his scissors right in front of the partner's nose, pretending that's what he'll do to him if he catches them together.'

" 'And Mom?' she asks.

" 'What about Mom?' I say, and now I'm getting a little cautious.

" 'Does she work at the hairdresser, too?'

" 'Of course not, she works at Taas, sorting ammo.' All of a sudden I feel like she's playing chess with me, each of us making our move and waiting to see what the other one will do.

" 'I didn't know they had women in Taas,' she says.

" 'They do,' I answer.

"She doesn't say anything. So I don't either. Then she asks if I want another cookie. I start thinking maybe the cookies are a move, too, and I'd best not take one, but I do take one and immediately I know it was a mistake. I don't know why, but it was a mistake.

" 'Eat up,' she says, sounding very pleased with herself. I put the cookie in my mouth and chew and I feel like throwing up. 'Do you have any brothers and sisters?' she asks.

"And by the way, we've long finished with the desert. There's green fields now, and regular cars, civilian ones, not army ones. I try to guess by the road signs how much longer to Jerusalem, but I don't know anything about all these intercity roads and I can't even figure out if we have an hour left, or half an hour, or three hours, and I don't want to ask. The sandwich and the egg keep repeating on me with the cookies.

"Let me tell you guys a joke," Dovaleh begs now, as if to say: I need a joke urgently, just a little one to sweeten my mouth. But two women at two different tables shout almost in unison: "Keep telling the story." They glance at each other awkwardly, and one gives her husband a sideways look. Dovaleh sighs, stretches, cracks his knuckles, takes a deep breath.

"And then the sister just throws out at me like it's nothing: 'And how are things for you with Dad? You get along, you two?'

"I remember my stomach turned over right then and there, and I just cut myself out of the place: I'm not here. I'm not anywhere. I'm not even allowed to be in any place. And you should know—open parentheses for a sec—that I have a thousand tricks for not being, I'm a world champion at not being, but all of a sudden I can't remember a single one of my tricks. I'm not kidding you. When he used to hit me, I'd practice stopping my heartbeat. I could get it down to twenty or thirty a minute, like I was hibernating, that's what I was aiming for, that was the dream. You'll think this is funny, but I also practiced spreading the pain out from the place that got hit to the other parts of my body, so it would be evenly divided—you know, equitable distribution of resources. While he was hitting I would imagine a column of ants coming to take the pain from my face or my stomach, and within seconds the ants would crumble it apart and move the crumbs to parts of my body that are more indifferent to pain."

He sways back and forth slightly, lost in himself. The light from above engulfs him in a misty veil. But then he opens his eyes and gives the little lady a long look, and then—he's doing it again—he moves his gaze to me with that same measured gesture, passing a flame from one candle to another. I still don't understand what he means by doing that, or what he's asking me to take from that woman, but I feel that he needs a token of approval from me, and I confirm with my eyes that he and she and I are holding some triangle of thread here, which perhaps one day I will understand.

"But his sister is just like him. Won't give up. 'I couldn't hear you,' she says and puts her hand on my shoulder, 'What was that?' I grip the door handle hard. What the hell is she doing putting her hand on me? And what's with all these questions? Maybe the driver does know something and he told her? My brain starts working overtime: How long was I actually asleep in the truck outside their house until they woke me? She had enough time to make the sandwiches and the hard-boiled eggs and the drinks, so maybe he stood next to her in the kitchen and told her everything? Even things I still don't know? I feel nauseous again. If I open the door right here, I can roll over on the road, I'll get a little banged up, but then I'll run into the fields and they won't find me until after the funeral, and then everything will be over and I won't have to do anything, and anyway who said I have to do anything, and where did I get this idea that it's all on me? 'We're okay,' I tell her. 'We get along, but it's better with Mom.'

"Don't ask me why those words came out. I never told anyone in the world what things were like in our home, not ever, not even kids in class, not even my best friends, they didn't hear a word out of me, so what the hell am I doing pouring my heart out to a stranger? To a woman whose name I don't even know? And anyway, what business of hers is it who I get along with and who I'm not so hot with? I feel awful. My eyes go dim. I start thinking—don't laugh now—that maybe there was something in her cookies that makes you talk, like in a police interrogation, until you confess."

Sleepwalking terror on his face: he's there. All of him is there.

"And the driver says to her quietly, 'Leave him alone, maybe he doesn't wanna talk about that now.' 'Of course he does,' she says. 'What else do you think he can talk about at a time like this? About monkeys in Africa? About your lamebrain jokes? Isn't that right, kid? Don't you want to talk about it?' She leans over and puts her hand on my shoulder again, and I smell something familiar, but I can't place it, some kind of sweet perfume coming from her, or maybe it's from the baby, and I breathe it in deeply, and I tell her yes.

"'I told you,' she says and tugs his ear hard, and he shouts 'Ouch!' and grabs his ear, and I remember thinking that, even though they fought a lot, you could tell they were siblings, and it sucked that I didn't have any. And the other thing that's in my head the whole time is that she knew her brother who died, the one the driver never knew. How can she manage to hold both of them in her mind?"

He pauses and looks at the little lady. She yawns repeatedly, rests her head on both hands, but her eyes are wide open and she watches him with intention and effort. He sits down at the edge of the stage with his legs dangling. The blood from his nose has congealed on his mouth and chin and painted two stripes on his shirt.

"I remember everything suddenly. That's what's amazing about this evening. I want you to know. You've done a great thing for me today by staying. I suddenly remember everything, and not in my sleep but like it's happening right now, this minute. For example, I remember sitting in the truck thinking that until we get there I have to be like an animal that doesn't understand anything about human life. A monkey or an ostrich or a fly, just as long as I don't understand any human speech or behavior. And I mustn't think. The most important thing now is to not think about anyone and not to want anything or anyone. Except that maybe I can think a few good things. But what would be considered a good thing now? Good for him? Good for her? I'm dead scared of making the tiniest mistake."

With effort he manages a crooked smile. His upper lip is very swollen, and his speech is getting more and more slurred.

"Where was I . . . ," he murmurs. "Where was I . . ."

No one answers. He sighs and goes on.

"I suddenly got the idea of thinking about a soft-boiled egg. Don't look at me like that. When I was little I couldn't stand eating soft-boiled eggs, the runny stuff made me gag, and the two of them would get mad and say I had to eat it, that all the vitamins were in that part, and there was yelling and slapping. Where food was concerned, by the way, she had no qualms about hitting. In the end, when nothing else worked, they'd tell me that if I didn't eat my egg they'd leave the house and never come back. But I still wouldn't eat it. So they'd put their coats on and pick up the key and stand in the doorway saying goodbye. And scared as I was to be left alone, I still didn't eat it. I don't know where I got the guts to stand up to them, and I argued, too, playing for time, and I just wanted it to stay like that forever, with them standing next to each other and talking to me, both the same way . . ."

He smiles to himself. He seems to be shrinking, his legs swinging in the air.

"So this is what I'm thinking about the soft egg: that maybe it's something I should see, just that, over and over and over again until we get there, like a movie with a happy ending. I happen to look in the rearview mirror and I see that his sister's eyes are full of tears again. She's sitting there crying quietly. And then it really all comes up at once—the salami, the cookies, everything. I yell at the driver to stop—now! I jump out and puke my guts out on the front tire. I vomit out everything she fed me and it doesn't stop, there's more and more. My mother always holds my head when I throw up. First time in my life I'm throwing up on my own."

He touches his forehead lightly. Here and there a few men and women distractedly hold their hands up to their own foreheads. I do, too. There is a moment of peculiar silence. People are lost in themselves. My fingers read my forehead. It's not easy for me, this touch. In recent years I've been steadily losing my hair, and there's wrinkling. Furrows appearing. Like something is tattooing my forehead from the inside, limning straight lines and diamonds and squares. The forehead of a goring ox, Tamara would say if she saw it.

"Come on, come with me," he says, waking us up gently. "Come on, I'm getting back into the truck. She hands me a cloth diaper and tells me to wipe my face. The diaper is freshly laundered. It smells good. I put it over my face like a bandage"—he spreads his hands over his face—"and now it's her turn. I've left her alone for too long. Good things, good things about her. How she rubs Anuga hand cream into her skin, and the whole house fills with the smell, and her long fingers, and how she touches her cheek when she thinks and when she reads. And how she always holds her hands folded against one another so you can't see where they sewed her up. She's even careful around me, I've never been able to count whether she has six scars or seven. Sometimes it's six, sometimes seven. Now it's his turn. No, hers again. That's more urgent. She keeps disappearing. She doesn't have a drop of color. Completely white, like she hasn't an ounce of blood in her body. Like she's already given up, maybe lost faith in me because I didn't think hard enough about her. Why aren't I thinking harder? Why is it so hard for me to call up pictures of her? I want to, of course I want to, come on—"

He stops. His head is straight up and he has a tortured expression. A dark shadow slowly climbs up from inside him across his face, opens its mouth wide, takes in air, then dives back down. At that moment a thought ripens inside me: I want him to read what I'm planning to write this evening. I want him to have time to read it. I want it to be with him when he goes there. I hope that, in some way which I do not fully understand or even believe in, this thing I write will have some kind of existence there, too.

"But then the way she was always embarrassing me . . . ," he mumbles. "Always making scenes, screaming at night, crying at the window till the whole neighborhood woke up. I didn't tell you about all that, but it does need to be taken into account, it must be considered before handing down the verdict, and this is something I began to comprehend at a pretty young age: that she's best for me when she's at home, when she's shut up in the apartment with just me, and it's only me and her and our talk and our shows, and the books she used to translate for me from Polish. She read me Kafka for kids, and Odysseus and Raskolnikov . . ." He laughs softly. "At bedtime she'd tell me about Hans Castorp and Michael Kohlhaas and Alyosha, all the treasures, and she adapted them for my age, or usually not—adapting was not her strong suit—but things got hardest when she went out. The second she got anywhere near the door or the window I'd be on alert, I had actual heart palpitations, and awful pressure right here, in my belly—"

He puts his hand on his stomach. There is a longing in that small movement.

"What can I tell you, my head was exploding from the two of them, both together, her, too, because all of a sudden she finally woke up on me, like she realized her time was almost up and we'd be there soon and it was her last chance to influence me, so she started yelling, begging, reminding me of all kinds of things, I can't remember what they were, and then *he* brought up even more things, anytime she said one thing he'd come up with another two, and she's pulling me this way and he's pulling the other way, and the closer we get to Jerusalem, the crazier they get.

"Plug them up, plug them up," he mutters feverishly, "plug up all the holes in my body. If I shut my eyes they come in through my ears, if I shut my mouth they come in through my nose. They're shoving, yelling, driving me mad, like little kids, they scream at me, they cry—Me, me, me, pick me!"

His words are barely intelligible. I get up and move to a table nearer the stage. It's strange to see him from so close. For an instant, when he looks up, the spotlight creates an optical illusion, and a fifty-seven-year-old boy is reflected out of a fourteen-year-old man.

"Then suddenly, I swear, this is not imaginary, I hear the baby talking into my ear. But not like a baby talks, no, he was like someone my age or even older, and he says to me, just like this, very considered: 'You really have to make up your mind now, kid, because we'll be there soon.' And I think: I can't really have heard that. I pray to God that the driver and his sister didn't hear it. I shouldn't even have thoughts like that, God can strike you dead for something like that. And I start yelling: 'Can't you shut him up! Shut him up already!' Then everything goes quiet, and the driver and his sister don't say anything, like they're scared of me, and then the baby makes one single shout, but a regular baby's."

He takes another gulp from the flask and turns it over. A few drops drizzle onto the floor. He signals to Yoav, who goes over to the stage with a sour face and refills the flask from a bottle of Gato Negro. Dovaleh urges him to pour some more. The little group sitting at the bar, his longtime fans from Petach Tikva, take advantage of his distraction to slip away. I don't think he even notices. A dark-skinned man in an undershirt comes out of the kitchen, leans on the empty bar, and lights a cigarette.

During this lull, the woman with the silver hair and thin glasses looks over at me. Our eyes interweave for a long and slightly surprising moment.

"Friends, any chance you know why I'm telling you this story tonight? How we even got onto this?" He breathes heavily, his face burns an unnatural red. "It'll be over soon, don't worry, I can see the light."

He takes his glasses off and glances at me. I believe he is reminding me of his request: that thing that comes out of a person without his control. That's what he wanted me to tell him. It cannot be put into words, I realize, and that must be the point of it. And he asks with his eyes: But still, do you think everyone knows it? And I nod: Yes. And he persists: And the person himself, does he know what this one and only thing of his is? And I think: Yes. Yes, deep in his heart he knows.

"The driver took me home to Romema, but when I got out of

the truck a neighbor yelled out the window: 'Dovaleh, what are you doing here? Go quickly to Givat Shaul, you might still make it!' So we tear over from Romema to Givat Shaul, to the cemetery, it's not far, maybe fifteen minutes. We drive like crazy, speeding through red lights. I remember it was quiet in the car. No one said a word. And me—"

He stops. Takes a deep breath.

"In my heart, in my black heart, I started doing my reckoning. That's how it went. It was time for my accounting. My rotten little accounting."

He pauses again, sinks deeper and deeper into himself.

When he resurfaces, he is rigid and clenched.

"Douche bag. That's what I am. You remember that. Write it down, Your Honor, factor it in when you get to the sentencing stage. Yeah, you guys look at me now and you see a nice guy, a jolly old fellow, a laugh riot. But me, since that day, and to this day, I've always been a barely fourteen-year-old douche bag with shit where his soul should be, sitting in that truck doing his rotten accounting, and it's the most fucked-up, twisted accounting a person can make in his life. You won't believe what I put into that tally. I sneaked in the tiniest, dirtiest little things for those few minutes while we drove from my house to the cemetery. I totaled up the two of them and our whole life together in a petty cash account."

His face looks like someone is wringing it out with an iron hand. "And to tell you the truth? Up until that moment I didn't even know what a son of a thousand bitches I was. I didn't realize what kind of filth I had inside me until I became nothing but filth from top to bottom, and I learned what a person is and what he's worth. In a few minutes I grasped it all, I got it, I calculated it, my brain did the whole calculation in half a second—plus this, minus that, another minus, one more, and that's it, it's for life, and it doesn't come off and it won't ever come off."

His hands grip and twist each other. In the prevailing silence, I force myself to try and remember, or at least guess, where I was in those moments, at four o'clock in the afternoon, just as the military vehicle pulled up to the cemetery. Maybe I was coming back from the shooting range with the platoon. Or maybe we were practicing formations on the parade court. I need to understand what happened earlier that day, in the late-morning hours, when I saw him come back from the tent with the backpack, then follow the drill sergeant to the truck. Why didn't I get up and run to him? I should have run over to him, walked him to the truck, asked what happened. I was his friend, wasn't I?

"The driver flies, his whole body's pressing the wheel. Pale as a ghost. People in the cars next to us look at me. People on the street look. I could tell they all knew exactly where we were going and what was going through my heart. How did they know? I didn't know it myself yet, certainly not everything, because all that time I still kept doing my accounting, and every few seconds I'd remember another thing and another thing and I'd add it to my fucking list, my *selektzia*, right, left, left, left . . ."

He chuckles apologetically. Halts his head jerks with his hand.

"For the life of me I couldn't figure out how all these people on the street knew what I'd decided before I myself knew, and how they knew what a shit I was. I remember one old guy spat on the sidewalk when we drove past him, and a religious guy with sidelocks literally ran away from me when the driver stopped to ask him how to get to Givat Shaul. And a woman walking with her little boy turned his head away from me. It was all signs.

"And I remember that the driver, all the way to the cemetery, didn't look me in the eye or even turn his face halfway to me. His sister had all but disappeared. I couldn't hear her breathing. The baby, too. And it was because of the baby being so quiet that I starting wondering what was going on, what had I done, and why was everyone being like that?

"'Cause I realized something bad had happened on the last leg of the drive, from home to here, or maybe even from the minute I'd left Be'er Ora. But what? What had happened? And what did everyone want from me? I mean, it was just thoughts, just flies buzzing around my brain, and nothing could happen from thoughts, no one can control their thoughts, you can't stop your brain, or tell it to think only this or only that. Right?"

The room is quiet. He doesn't look up at us.

As if he is still afraid of the answer.

"And I couldn't understand it, I just couldn't, but I didn't have anyone to ask. I was alone. And all that stuff made a new thought settle down in my head: This must be it. It must have already happened. I've already given the verdict."

He stretches his arms up, then down, then out to the sides, searching for a way to breathe. He doesn't look at me, but I can feel that now, perhaps more than at any other moment this evening, he is asking me to see him.

"And the thing is, I didn't know how it got that way at all. I couldn't pinpoint where it had happened that I'd decided. I quickly tried to reverse what I thought, I swear I did, honestly, and anyway, what the fuck? Why the hell did I end up deciding that way? The whole time I'd had something completely different in my mind, my whole life I'd had something different, but then without even thinking—who the hell gives these things a second thought?" His voice cracks into a panicked scream. "And now this, all of a sudden? Why did I flip-flop at the last minute and decide the most opposite from what I really wanted? How could a whole lifetime flip over on me in one second just because of the stupid, random thoughts of a stupid kid . . ."

He plunges into the armchair.

"Those few moments," he murmurs, "and the whole drive, and the whole fucking accounting . . ." He turns his hands over slowly and examines his palms with a curiosity that embodies a lifetime. "Such dirt on me, such pollution . . . God, all the way to my bones . . ."

If I'd only stood up and run to him before he got into the truck and left. Even though it was in the middle of a lesson. Even though the sergeant was with him and would probably have yelled at me. Even though I have no doubt—and I guess I didn't have any then either—that everyone would have made fun of me for the rest of the camp. They'd have made me their punching bag. Instead of him.

He holds his head in his hands, pressing his temples. I don't know what he's thinking about now, but I pick myself up from the sandy quad and run to him. I can vividly remember the route. The path lined with whitewashed stones. The parade lot with the flag. The big army tents. The barracks. The sergeant shouting at me, threatening. I ignore him. I get to Dovaleh and walk beside him. He notices me and keeps walking, crushed under the weight of the backpack. He looks stunned. I reach out and touch his shoulder, and he stops and stares at me. Maybe he's trying to figure out what I want from him after everything that happened. What's the status between us now? I ask him: What happened? Where are they taking you? He shrugs his shoulders and looks at the drill sergeant and asks him what happened. And the drill sergeant answers him.

And if he doesn't answer, I ask Dovaleh again.

And he asks the drill sergeant.

And we do that until he answers.

"Sometimes I think the filth of that reckoning hasn't worked itself out of my blood to this day. And it can't. How could it? That kind of filth . . ." He searches for the right word, his fingers milking it out of the air: "It's radioactive. Yeah. My own private Chernobyl. A single moment that lasts a lifetime, still poisoning anything I come close to, to this day. Every person I touch."

The club is silent.

"Or marry. Or give birth to."

I turn and glance at the girl who was about to leave but stayed. She is weeping into her hands. Her shoulders shake.

"Go on," whispers a large woman with a mane of curls.

He stares out hazily in the direction of the voice, nodding wearily. Only now do I realize something invaluable: he has not given a single hint, this entire evening, that I was there with him at the camp. He hasn't turned me in.

"What more is there to tell. We got to Givat Shaul, and that place is a conveyor belt, a factory, three funerals an hour, *bam-bam-bam,* how you gonna find the right one? We parked on the sidewalk, left the sister and her baby in the pickup, and me and the driver took off in a mad rush all over the place.

"And don't forget it's my first funeral. I didn't even know where to look or what to look for or where the person who died is supposed to be, where's he gonna come from suddenly, and whether you can see him or if he's covered. I saw people standing around in groups, each group in a different area, and I didn't know what they were waiting for or who was in charge or what we were supposed to do.

"Then I saw this Bulgarian redhead, and I knew he worked with Dad, he supplied lotions and shampoos, and next to him was a woman who worked at Taas, a shift manager who Mom was dead scared of, and a little behind them I saw Silviu, Dad's partner, with a bunch of flowers in his hand.

"I told the driver that was it and he stood still, gave me some distance, said something like 'Be tough, kid.' And the truth is, it was hard for me to leave him. I don't even know his name. If he happens to be here tonight, could he raise his hand? He'll get a free drink on the house, eh?"

Judging by his strained, stubborn look, he seems to honestly believe it's a possibility.

"Where are you?" He snorts. "Where are you, my righteous comic brother, who told me jokes the whole way and lied about the joke contest? I looked into it a while ago. I'm doing some housecleaning, you know, tying up loose ends. I asked around, made some inquiries, I googled, I looked through old issues of *Bamahaneh*, but there was no such thing, ever, no joke contest in the army, he just made it up for me, that sneaky Jokerman. Wanted to soften the blow a little. Where are you, my good man?

"Now stay with me, don't let go of my hand for a second.

The driver went back to the pickup, and I walked over to the people standing around. I remember walking slowly, like I was stepping on broken glass, but my eyes raced around like crazy. There's a neighbor from our building, the lady who always fights with us 'cause all the rags we hang out to dry drip on her laundry, and now she's here. And there's the doctor who does cupping on Dad when he has high blood pressure, and there's the woman from Mom's shtetl who brings her books in Polish, and there's that guy, and there's that other woman.

"There were maybe twenty of them. I didn't know we knew so many people. Hardly anyone spoke to us around the neighborhood. Maybe they were from the barbershop? I don't know. I didn't go near them. I couldn't see him or her. Then a few people caught sight of me and they pointed and whispered. I let the backpack slide off my body. I didn't have the strength to carry anything anymore."

He hugs his body.

"Suddenly a tall guy with a black-broom beard from Chevra Kadisha comes over to me and says, 'Are you the orphan? Are you the Greenstein orphan? Where were you? We've been waiting for you!' He grabs my hand, hard, like he wants to strangle it, and pulls me with him. As we walk, he sticks a cardboard yarmulke on my head—"

Dovaleh locks onto me now with his eyes. I give him everything I have and everything I don't have.

"He rushed me to this stone building, took me inside. I didn't look. I shut my eyes. I thought maybe Mom or Dad would be there, waiting. Thought I'd hear my name. In her voice or his. But I didn't hear anything. I opened my eyes. They weren't there. Just a big religious guy with his sleeves rolled up rushing along the side of the room carrying a shovel. The one with the beard dragged me across the room and through another door. I was in a smaller room now, with big sinks on one side, and a bucket and some towels or wet sheets. There was a long sort of trolley with a bundle laid on it, wrapped in white fabric, and then I realized that was it: there was a person in there. The guy says to me: 'Ask for forgiveness.' But I—"

Dovaleh drops his head to his chest, hugging himself tightly.

"I didn't move. So he poked his finger into my shoulder from behind: 'Ask for forgiveness.' I said, 'Ask who?' And I didn't look in that direction, except that suddenly I got a thought in my head that it actually wasn't a very long bundle, so maybe it wasn't her—it wasn't her! Maybe I was just scared, my mind playing tricks on me. And then I felt happier than I've ever felt in my life, before or since. It was a wild happiness, like I myself had been saved from death. He shoved me on the shoulder again: 'Go on, ask for forgiveness.' So I asked again: 'But from who?' And then the penny dropped and he stopped prodding me and asked, 'Don't you know?' I said I didn't. And he panicked: 'They didn't tell you?' Again I said no. He crouched down to my level, and I saw his eyes opposite mine, and he said, quietly and gently, 'But this is your mother here.'

"And then what do I remember? I remember . . . I do, I wish I didn't remember so much, maybe there'd be space left in my mind for other things. The Chevra Kadisha guy quickly takes me back to the big room, and the people I'd seen outside were gathered in the room now, and when I walked inside the crowd parted, and I saw my father leaning on his partner's shoulder, he could barely stand on his own feet, he hung like a baby on Silviu and didn't even see me. And I thought . . . what did I think . . ."

He takes a deep breath. Far deeper than the depth of his body.

"I thought I should go up and hug him. But I couldn't go,

and I definitely couldn't look in his eyes. People behind me said, 'Go on, go to Dad, go on already, *kaddishel*, you have to say the prayers,' and Silviu whispered to him that I was there, and he looked up and his eyes opened wide like he'd seen the Messiah. He let go of Silviu and wobbled over to me with his arms open and he shouted and cried out her name and my name together. He looked suddenly old, wailing in Yiddish in front of everyone about how it was just the two of us now, and how could such a catastrophe have befallen us, and why did we deserve it, we never hurt anyone. I didn't move, I didn't take a step toward him. I just looked at his face and thought what an idiot he was for not understanding that it could have been the complete opposite—one single millimeter this way or that and it could have been the opposite. And I thought: If he hugs me now or even just touches me I'll hit him, I'll kill him, I can do it, I'm all-powerful, everything I say comes true. And the second I had that thought, my body flipped me upside down. Flung me up, threw me on my hands, the yarmulke fell off, and I heard everyone breathing and it went quiet.

"I started running away, and he ran after me, and he still didn't understand and he shouted in Yiddish for me to stop, to come back, but it was all upside down with me, I made everything upside down. I could see from the bottom how all the people made way when I walked through them, and I left the room and no one had the guts to stop me. He ran after me and yelled and cried, until he stopped in the doorway. I stopped, too, in the parking lot, and we stood there looking at each other, me this way and him the other way, and then I saw for real that he wasn't worth anything without her, and that all his power in life came from her being with him. He turned into half a human in that one instant.

"He looked at me, I saw his eyes slowly get closer together, and I had the clear sense that he was beginning to understand. I don't know how, but he had animal instincts about that kind of thing. You'll never convince me he didn't. In that one second, he grasped everything I'd done on the way, my whole lousy accounting. He read it all on my face in one second. He held both hands up, and I think—no, I'm sure—he cursed me. Because what came out of his mouth was a shout I've never heard come out of a human being. It sounded like I'd killed him. And I fell down that very minute. My hands buckled and I flattened on the asphalt.

"People in the parking lot looked at us. I don't know what he said to me, what the curse was, maybe it was all in my head, but I saw his face and I could feel it was one hell of a curse, and at that point I still didn't know it would hold up my whole life, but that's how it was, everywhere I went, anywhere I ran.

"Listen to this: that was the first time it went through my mind that maybe I hadn't understood anything, and that he really was prepared to lie on that gurney in her place. When it came to her, he didn't do any accounting. He really did love her."

His body goes limp. "Well, of course . . . ," he murmurs and fades away for a long minute.

"Then he did this to me with his hand—he gave up on me. He turned and went back inside to continue the funeral, and I got up and ran through the people and the cars, and I knew then that that was it, I wouldn't be going home. Home was shut for me."

He slowly puts the flask down by his feet. His head droops forward as it did when he began the story.

"Where could I go? Who was waiting for me? I spent the first night in the school basement, and the second night in the synagogue storeroom, and on the third night I crawled home with my tail between my legs. And he opened the door for me. He didn't say a word. He made me dinner as usual, but without talking, either to me or to himself."

Dovaleh straightens up. His head sways on his thin neck.

"And that's how our life after her began. Me and him, alone. But that'll have to wait for another evening. I'm a little tired now."

Silence. No one moves.

A minute passes, then another. The manager looks right, left, clears his throat, slaps his fleshy thighs with both hands, stands up, and starts stacking chairs. People get up and quietly leave without looking at one another. Here and there a woman gives Dovaleh a subtle nod. His face is extinguished. The tall silver-haired woman approaches the stage and bows her head at him. When she passes me on her way out, she puts a folded note on my table. I notice the laugh lines around her tearful eyes.

Then only the three of us are left. The little woman clutches her red purse with both hands, standing next to her chair and leaning on one leg. She is so tiny, little Eurycleia. She waits, looking at him hopefully. He slowly comes back from the place he sank into, looks up at her, and smiles.

"Good night, Pitz," he says. "Don't stay here. And don't walk home either. This isn't a good area. Yoav!" he calls to the lobby. "Call her a cab! Take it off my fee if there's anything left."

She doesn't move. She's planted herself there.

He gets down heavily from the stage and stands facing her. He's even shorter than he appeared onstage. He leans over with old-fashioned, knightly grace and kisses her on the cheek, then takes a step back. She still doesn't move. She stands on her tip-toes, eyes shut, her whole body pulling toward him. He moves closer again and kisses her on the lips.

"Thanks, Pitz," he says, "thanks for everything. You have no idea."

"You're welcome," she says with that matter-of-fact serious-ness, but her face is flushed and her birdlike chest swells. She turns and walks out with a slight limp, her lips rounded into a smile of pure joy.

Now it's just me and him in the club. He stands facing me, leaning one hand on the edge of my table, and I sit down imme-diately so as not to distress him with the mass of my body.

"I sentence you now to death by drowning!" he says, quoting the father to his son from Kafka's story, then holds the flask up over his head and drizzles the last few drops on himself. A few of them fall on me. The dark-skinned man in the undershirt is back in the kitchen washing dishes, belting out "Let It Be."

"Do you have another minute?" His arms shake with effort as he hoists himself back onto the stage and sits on the edge.

"Even an hour."

"You're not in a rush to get home?"

"I'm not in a rush to get anywhere."

"Just, you know . . ." He smiles feebly. "Just till the adrena-line goes down a bit."

His head is on his chest. He looks like he's fallen asleep sit-ting up.

Suddenly Tamara is here, all around me. I feel her presence with such force that I have to hold my breath. I tune in to her and I can hear her whisper in my ear, quoting our beloved Fer-nando Pessoa: "To be whole, it is enough to exist."

Dovaleh shakes himself awake and opens his eyes. It takes him a minute to adjust his pupils. "I saw you were scribbling a bit," he says.

"I thought I might try and write something up."

"Really?" His face fills with a smile.

"When it's finished, I'll give it to you."

"At least there'll be a few words left behind." He laughs awkwardly. "Like sawdust, you know . . ."

"It's funny," he says afterward and dusts his hands off. "I'm not a person who misses . . . anyone."

That surprises me, but I don't say anything.

"But tonight, I don't know . . . Maybe for the first time since she died . . ." He runs a finger over the glasses lying on the stage floor. "I had some moments when I really felt her . . . Not just like my mother, I mean, but like a human being. One human being who was here in the world. Dad kept going almost thirty years after her, you know? For the last few years I took care of him. At least he died at home, with me."

"You mean in Romema?"

He shrugs his shoulders. "I didn't get very far."

I see him and his father passing each other in the hall. Dusty time piles up over them.

"How about you let me take you home?" I suggest.

He thinks for a moment. Shrugs again. "If you insist."

"Go get ready," I say, standing up. "I'll wait outside."

"Wait, not so fast. Sit down. Be an audience for one more second."

He puffs up his chest and cups his hands around his mouth

like a megaphone: "Show's over, Caesarea!" From the edge of the stage he sends me his most glowing smile. "That's all I have to give you. There's no more Dovaleh being given out today, and there won't be tomorrow either. This concludes the ceremonials. Please be careful on your way out. Pay attention to the ushers and security personnel. I'm told there's heavy traffic at the exits. Good night, everyone."

FALLING OUT OF TIME

In this compassionate and genre-defying drama, the internationally acclaimed David Grossman weaves an incandescent tale of parental grief. A powerful distillation of the experience of understanding and acceptance, and of art's triumph over death, *Falling Out of Time* is part play, part prose, and pure poetry. As Grossman's characters ultimately find solace and hope through their communal acts of mourning, readers will find comfort in their clamorous vitality, and in the gift of storytelling—a realm where loss is not an absence, but a life force in its own right.

Fiction/Literature

TO THE END OF THE LAND

Just before his release from service in the Israeli army, Ora's son Ofer is sent back to the front for a major offensive. In a fit of preemptive grief and magical thinking, so that no bad news can reach her, Ora sets out on an epic hike in the Galilee. She is joined by an unlikely companion—Avram, a former friend and lover with a troubled past—and as they sleep out in the hills, Ora begins to conjure her son. Ofer's story, as told by Ora, becomes a surprising balm both for her and for Avram—and a mother's powerful meditation on war and family.

Fiction/Literature

VINTAGE INTERNATIONAL
Available wherever books are sold.
www.vintagebooks.com